HUNGRY AS HER PYTHON

HUNGRY FUR LOVE
BOOK 3

C.D. GORRI

To everyone who believed in and supported my Kickstarter to relaunch this series. I am so grateful for your trust and faith.

To everyone I've met in my travels at reader cons and book signings, thank you for being the best cheerleaders a writer from New Jersey could ever have! Your support means the world to me.

And of course, I have to say thanks to all of you fantastic readers.

Holy cow, do you rock!

Thank you for allowing me to share my Castor's Corner Witch Trifecta with you. I hope you find these stories entertaining, and that they make you LOL.

The Hungry Fur Love stories began as a lighthearted pun, but these three Witches have captured my heart—with any luck they'll reach you, too. Thank you for visiting my Jersey Shore, we're gonna do great things here.

Happy reading!

del mare alla stella,
C.D. Gorri

HUNGRY AS HER PYTHON
HUNGRY FUR LOVE 3 COPYRIGHT

By C.D. Gorri
Edited by BookNookNuts
Copyright © 2022, 2025

HUNGRY FUR LOVE

THE SERIES

Welcome to Castor's Corner—where the witches are curvy, the magic is unpredictable, and the fated mates come with fur, fangs, and deliciously dirty minds.

The witch trifecta of Castor's Corner is made up of three over-thirty besties who might be a magical mess, but they've got hearts of gold and zero time for nonsense—unless it comes in the form of a smoldering supernatural male.

As the guardians of their quirky, chaos-prone town, these witches are supposed to keep things under control.

Then the barrier goes down, and all magical hell breaks loose.

Now the town's crawling with trouble: ghouls in

the cemetery, talking pets with attitude, ghostly family drama, and worst of all—gorgeous shifters who might just be their fated mates.

These sexy strangers are growly, protective, and utterly devoted. And they're not backing off, no matter how messy things get.

If you love:

✔ Fated mates who can't resist a curvy witch

✔ Magical mischief and hilarious spell fails

✔ Steamy slow burns with a side of claws and cuddles

✔ Found family, fierce friendship, and paranormal chaos

Then buckle up, buttercup. The Hungry Fur Love series is here to cast a spell on your heart—and maybe your underwear.

Dive into this sizzling romcom series full of heart, heat, and happily-ever-afters with bite today!

HUNGRY AS HER PYTHON

A Curvy Witch Meets Patient Python Shifter Fated Mates Romance

A curvy Witch, a sinfully smooth Python Shifter, and one naked bonfire away from getting scorched.

Will I ever learn to trust my magic, my instincts, and my heart?

Growing up Witchy in Castor's Corner has always been a mixed bag of perks and pains.

Perk #1: I run a magical bakery in a town full of supernatural sweet tooths.

Drawback #1: Supernatural metabolism? Totally skipped me and my two cousins.

Perk #2: I test new spells and recipes every day. The treats are dangerously delicious.

Drawback #2: They never do what I want—unless gaining a few extra curves counts as spell success.

Still, I own every inch of me. Mom always says curvy is as curvy does—and I do curvy damn well.

As one-third of our Witchy Trifecta, my job is to help keep Castor's Corner safe from supernatural shenanigans. But ever since we let our magical guard down, things have been a little wild.

My cousins found their fated mates, the town's crawling with Shifters, and even our grumpy Ghost Grandpa seems to be glowing.

Me? I'm still single, still baking, and still pretending I don't have it bad for Conrad Boman—an insanely sexy Python Shifter who looks at me like I'm the only dessert on the menu.

With the Summer Solstice around the corner, my plate is officially full.

Finish the perfect cake for my besties' double wedding.

Find out who's setting fires in my bakery.

Survive the monthly naked bonfire casting party.

Try not to fall tail-over-teakettle for a man who coils when he's flustered

June is heating up fast—and this curvy little baker might just be ready to take the leap.

All I have to do is trust myself, and maybe let the Snake in.

PROLOGUE-BELLA

EVERYTHING *GOOD STARTS* with a leap of faith.

At least, that's what I've learned.

But whoever came up with that cute little Pinterest quote probably wasn't talking about diving headfirst into a relationship with a giant, smug Shifter who kisses like sin and rearranges your whole life just by looking at you.

Or about running a bakery in a magical town where the probability of a fire, curse, or spontaneous goat stampede is higher than the odds of a cake rising evenly.

Still, I guess I've always been the leap-first, pray-later type.

I wasn't born that way, though.

Once upon a time, I was the opposite.

Quiet.

Timid.

Downright shy.

I was the little Witch who always sat in the back of the classroom, clutching my spell primer like a shield and hoping no one noticed me—*because if they didn't notice me, they couldn't laugh when my magic fizzled or went sideways, especially when I tried to increase whatever my mom had packed for snack time.*

I still remember that first day at the Castor's Corner Preschool, where most gifted young Witches went.

My hair was in two braids so tight my scalp ached, my shoes were new and pinched my toes, and I was so sure I'd spend the day hiding behind the potted asphodel in the corner until Mommy came to take me home.

And then *they* walked in.

Donny, with her wild curls, paint-smeared dress, and big eyes, like she already knew every secret worth knowing. And Evie, in a sparkly cape she'd borrowed from her older cousin, marching in like she already ran the place—*as she would inevitably run the whole town.*

They plopped down on either side of me without

so much as a *"Can I sit here?"* and started chattering like we'd been friends forever.

Donny showed me how to charm the class crayons into coloring by themselves. Evie slipped me one of the gummy frogs she'd smuggled in her pocket and swore she'd hex anyone who tried to mess with me.

By the end of that first morning, I wasn't hiding anymore.

I was laughing.

I was belonging.

That leap of faith—*letting them both in*—changed my life.

Fast forward a couple of decades, and here we are.

Still besties.

Still causing trouble.

Still saving each other when the cauldron boils over—sometimes literally.

We were the Witch Trifecta of Castor's Corner—*capital T, like it was an official title, which in a way, it kind of was.*

Three Witches.

Three different specialties.

Three very different personalities.

Evie Castor was our fearless mayor-slash-over-worked miracle worker, all polished poise and political charm—*until you put her in a kitchen, then it was may the Goddess help us all.*

Donny Andrews was the bold, brash, curse-like-a-sailor hair magician with a flair for drama and an entire drawer of battery-operated stress relievers she'd recently retired when she mated a certain big Bear Shifter who occasionally worked for me and made the best croissants ever.

It was the hands. The man had enormous hands and rolled out a thousand layers faster than my magic could.

But what did you expect? He was a Grizzly Bear, for Pete's sake!

There was simply no comparison.

And then there was me—*Bella Strega.*

Baker extraordinaire, Kitchen Witch, and the glue that kept us together, mostly because I bribed them with marshmallow frosted cupcakes.

We didn't do things the same way—*not even close.*

Evie planned.

Donny improvised.

I typically winged it with a smile and a pastry box.

But somehow, it worked. It had always worked.

And I never wanted it to change.

Except, well, change was inevitable, wasn't it?

Like accidentally baking your emotions into a batch of muffins—*you didn't mean to do it, but there they were, puffed up and impossible to ignore.*

True friendships endured, at least that's what they say.

And mine with Evie and Donny? Unshakable.

If the world ended tomorrow, I'd be passing out sugar cookies while Evie organized the evacuation routes and Donny hexed anyone who got in our way.

But this past year?

Oh boy.

We'd had more disruptions to our cozy little slice of South Jersey than in the entire decade before combined.

First came those darned Shifters, wandering into town like the world's hottest lost-and-found items.

One minute we were minding our business (if Evie being late to our bonfire was minding our own business, then yeah, let's go with that), the next minute—*bam*—walking, talking Shifter-sized sex dolls claiming to be our fated mates started popping up everywhere.

Okay, there were only three of them, but sheesh, they were big.

Anyway, then Grandpa Al's ghost decided the cemetery was the perfect place for a long-term staycation.

And just when we thought we'd seen it all, Magdelena—*La Befana, the supreme Witch in these parts who worked directly under the magic-freaking-master Morrigan herself*—gifted us three familiars so strange they made even me question the ingredients for my go to chocolate chip pumpkin muffins with chocolate cream cheese frosting.

And trust me, I've made those blindfolded wearing nothing but a sequined apron after an all-night Hex & Mingle party over at Castor's Bar on Woodlock Lane.

So, yeah. We'd been busy.

But if I'm going to tell you the latest story—*the one where things went sideways faster than Donny at a clearance sale at Sephora*—then we have to roll the clock back.

To the exact moment when the magically mischievous shit hit the metaphorical fan.

And spoiler alert, it wasn't pretty.

It never was.

Unless you count the sexy Snake Shifter who was right smack dab in the middle of it all.

Palm Sunday–One Week Before Easter

The fire alarm had finally stopped screaming, but my head was still ringing like church bells on a wedding day.

And not in any *they lived happily ever after* romantic way.

Nope. It was more like the *your life is in smoldering ruins* kind of way.

I stood in the middle of my shop, staring at the wreckage in total denial.

Broken glass glittered across the floor like some tragic disco ball.

Display cases were toppled, their contents drowned in puddles of dirty water.

My specialty chocolate bunnies had melted into grotesque little blobs.

The Easter *panettone*? Burned to the kind of crisp that would shatter teeth.

And my egg-shaped cupcakes looked like they'd gone through a demolition derby.

Weeks of work—*undone.*

Endless hours of baking and chocolate molding —*wasted.*

All those specialty ingredients I only got once a year—*poof, gone!*

Easter was ruined.

And I was in emotional shambles.

Why me? Why my shop?

Despair roared to life in my chest, and I wanted to weep.

Now that the danger was over, the adrenaline was crashing hard, leaving me with nothing but the smoke, the soggy mess, and the ugly truth that I was going to have to clean all this up before I could even think about baking again.

Luckily, my familiar was already on it.

Petyr was good like that.

Unfortunately, I was magically bound to only use my Witchcraft in the bakery kitchen itself, which was currently a no-go zone until the mess was cleared.

Petyr, however, had no such limitations. The furry little Domovyk could cast wherever and whenever—though his idea of *help* was often chaotic at best.

"Bella? Hey, I just wanted to give you an update. The fire is out, but the cause is still a mystery. I'll be back in a few to help with the cleanup," Ryan called from the doorway, already climbing back into the big red fire engine.

His flannel was streaked with soot, his hair damp from the spray. The man might be a Grizzly Bear Shifter, but in that moment, he was a firefighter and the savior of my store.

He was also mated to my bestie and cousin, Donny, and he worked as my part-time employee.

I was seriously grateful for all his help, I just did not have the energy to show it right then.

"I'll be here," I sang back, trying not to sound defeated.

He was headed back to the Castor's Corner Firehouse, probably to file reports or scrub soot off the gear. I didn't ask.

The smoke was stinging my eyes, and my throat felt like I'd swallowed a handful of cinders.

Stinking firebug.

Someone was doing this on purpose.

To me.

I could feel it in my flour-dusted bones. And if I had to hex every last troublemaker in town to find them, I would.

"Petyr? You finished?" I rasped, stepping inside.

"Da, my Witchy. You come now," he said from right beside me.

I jumped.

"How in the world—"

A coughing fit cut me off, and Petyr held up a bottle of water.

"Cold will not work," I waved him off. "I need hot tea. Possibly with brandy. Heavy on the brandy."

Before Petyr could answer, a car pulled into the lot behind me.

My familiar's little horned head tilted toward the sound, and he muttered, "He is here."

Of course he was.

I closed my eyes, willing the intruder away. No such luck.

Six and a half feet of gorgeous, trouble-making man unfolded from the patrol car, all lazy grace, and broad shoulders.

Conrad moved like steam—rising, curling, filling the space between us without touching me.

One second, he was across the parking lot and the next, poof, right in front of me.

"Are you alright?" he asked, and his voice wrapped around me like warm honey with a bite of heat at the end.

Petyr squinted up at him, snarling before glancing back at me.

"Want me to get rid?"

I shook my head slightly at his offer.

"Uh, yeah, I'm fine. Thank you for coming," I said, already regretting it.

The last time I'd seen Conrad, we'd both been coming.

Hard.

Simultaneously.

And ever since, I'd been steering clear like a Witch who knows better than to look into a cursed mirror—*nothing good ever comes out of it.*

I turned around, ready to dismiss him, but of course, the Shifter was having none of that.

"It's time we talk, Maribella," he said, using that full-name tone that made my spine tingle.

I crossed my arms, desperate for armor.

"Look, Conrad, I'm sorry you caught feelings. I told you then—it was just one night. You're a big boy. I shouldn't have to explain this to you."

A slow grin curved his mouth, and his cheeks darkened with what might have been embarrassment—*if I believed for a second that Conrad was capable of being embarrassed.*

Hint: He wasn't.

"I meant about the fire, Sugar. But if there's something else on your mind, I'm all ears."

And there it was.

The sexy eyebrow raise.

The slow once-over that lingered on my soot-smeared apron and hair.

Well, crap. I walked right into that one.

"I'll call Jaxson later with my statement. Good-bye, deputy," I muttered, pushing past him before I could dig myself deeper.

Behind me, Petyr let out a low snort.

"You like him."

"I do not."

"You do."

"Petyr, I swear on the Goddess's cupcake stand, I will turn you into a fuzzy throw pillow."

Worst. Day. Ever. And it was only just starting.

CHAPTER ONE-BELLA

OKAY, so Spring in Castor's Corner used to be my absolute favorite season.

Call me crazy, but I loved the mood swings of Mother Earth during that time of year.

Hot, cold, dry, wet.

Like she was throwing climate tantrums, and I was here for it.

It made me feel connected somehow. Just knowing that I wasn't the only hot mess around kinda helped, I guess.

Technically, Palm Sunday was a disaster, but by the time Easter had come and gone, I'd managed to salvage some treats and chocolates for the actual holiday.

Fact was, I put that fire out of my mind almost as

soon as it happened.

I mean, I'd thought I'd already seen the worst of Spring on that cold, crappy morning.

Oh, but bless my clueless heart, I was wrong.

Between Mother Nature's bipolar disorder and not knowing what natural, *or unnatural*, disaster might strike next, well, let's just say my closet was a fabric avalanche waiting to happen.

I had short, flowy dresses tangling with thick sweaters and flannels, and all of it was mixed up with my plethora of pink chef's pants.

This time of year, you kinda needed to be ready for anything.

And believe me, I thought I was.

Anyway, I wasn't about to put away my cozy knits just to get frostbite when April decided to pull a fast one.

But the truth was just lately?

The cute unpredictability of the weather had lost its charm.

We had five inches of snow in the last week of March.

Then a hurricane in mid-April that smacked our shoreline like it had a personal vendetta.

The week after that?

Eighty-degree heat for five days straight, sending

everyone scrambling for their window AC units—only for the temperature to plummet back into the fifties overnight.

May was a dreary, wet, muddy mess.

And now, with June here, I was starting to wonder if summer had Ghosted us entirely.

Normally, I loved the not-knowing.

It kept things interesting.

But lately, I'd been off my game.

Restless. Like my magic was sitting just under my skin, waiting for trouble.

And Castor's Corner always, always, delivered on trouble.

"Maribella Strega, keep it together," I muttered, massaging my temples.

Where had it all gone sideways?

But that question was rhetorical.

I knew exactly when, where, how and most importantly who.

Less than a year ago, I was plain old Bella—owner of The Tasty Tart bakery, proud member of the town's Witch Trifecta, and reigning blueberry pie queen of the Summer Solstice Festival.

My life was predictable in the best way—sugar, spells, and Saturdays with my girls.

Then Evie was late to our monthly bonfire where

we recharged the town's wards, and everything went straight to Hell in a magical handbasket.

Kidnappings.

Cemetery hauntings.

An evil Warlock trying to take over.

The Chicky twins hexing Grandpa Al's remains and hoarding hair clippings to control half the town like some kind of dark-magic HOA.

It was like living in the Witchy Wild West—*gunslingers swapped for spell-slingers.*

Things had quieted down since then. Well, for a while, they had.

But Castor's Corner trouble is like a hydra—*you cut off one head, and two more sprout up, usually carrying pitchforks and a curse.*

Let me back up and give you the quick-and-dirty history.

Castor's Corner is home.

Always has been.

This tiny coastal New Jersey town has been a supernatural safe haven since the U.S. flag only had thirteen stars.

Our founding Witches laid down wards so strong they nudge humans away from our borders without them ever realizing it.

And me? I share a bloodline with two of the most powerful women in town—Evie and Donny.

We found out we were cousins not too long ago.

It was the kind of soap-opera twist that made my mom clutch her pearls, but I thought it was awesome.

Our mutual grandfather, Al Castor, was a total dog—literally and magically.

He strayed outside his marriage and fathered at least two illegitimate kids, one of them my dad, the other Donny's.

Magical men. They're charming until they're not.

Mostly not.

Which is exactly why I'm single.

Okay, partly.

The other reason is that once your heart's been drop-kicked into oblivion, you get a little gun-shy.

Fool me once, shame on you.

Fool me twice? Not happening, Buster.

Besides, my life is full—baking, casting, and hanging with my girls.

What else does a Witch need?

Okay, fine.

Maybe I missed having someone to keep the bed warm.

But options? I had them.

Plenty of them.

I just wasn't biting.

Well. Not unless you counted *him.*

Which I didn't.

"The glass is gone," Petyr grumbled, dragging me out of my mental spiral.

"Thanks, Petyr," I said, patting his shaggy head.

My Domovyk familiar was all big eyes and bigger attitude.

We'd clicked instantly, unlike Evie and Donny with theirs.

Honestly, I think that was their fault, not the familiars'.

"You're welcome, my Witchy," he said, hauling a trash bag to the dumpster like a furry little mafia enforcer.

I sighed.

Time to see what I could salvage from the latest disaster.

I'd just had the whole store repainted after the Palm Sunday fire, and here we were again—a few days away from the Summer Solstice Bash and some firebug had decided my bakery was a repeat target.

You heard me.

We'd been hit.

Again.

My phone buzzed with texts from Evie and Donny, both offering to come down. But why should they? What could they do?

So, no, I didn't answer.

This was small scale compared to some of the messes we'd handled.

I wasn't dragging them out of bed at 2 AM for a little mess.

Okay, fine, it was more than a little mess.

But it was *mine* to handle, and I was a big girl now.

"What else could go wrong?" I muttered.

And right on cue, the Fates heard me and cackled.

A patrol car rolled into the lot, and like an instant replay of what happened on Palm Sunday, six and a half feet of trouble unfolded from the driver's seat.

Broad shoulders.

Blond hair.

Eyes that could hypnotize a girl into making very, very bad decisions.

Plus, he wore a concerned expression that made me want to kick him in the shins.

The snake! Pun intended.

I groaned. "Of course it's you."

Because my girly bits clearly hadn't gotten the memo about my no dating Shifters policy—they perked up like he was bringing cupcakes and an apology.

Memories from our night together—*sweaty skin, his low growl, the way his hands owned me*—flashed, and I had to lock my knees to keep from puddling at his boots.

"Can I have a moment, Maribella?" Conrad asked, his voice a deep rumble.

And just like that, I remembered exactly why I didn't trust springtime in Castor's Corner.

Or myself.

I pursed my lips and waited, because if I opened my mouth too soon, something stupid was bound to come out.

Last time Conrad had shown up here in uniform, I'd made the catastrophic mistake of thinking he wanted to talk about us—*or rather, the utter lack of an us*—because I'd shut him down more times than a health inspector in a cursed kitchen.

Egads. The man was so freaking hot it ought to be illegal.

CHAPTER TWO—BELLA

THOSE EMERALD EYES of his glittered in the overhead light as he raked his gaze over me from head to toe.

I didn't want to think about what I looked like—hair mussed from smoke and wind, soot streaks on my cheek, probably flour somewhere it shouldn't be.

And here he was, looking outrageously good despite the ungodly hour.

Was it possible he'd gotten even more handsome since the last time I saw him?

Because I was ninety percent sure that was illegal under some magical treaty.

And it was so damn unfair that male Shifters—*and men in general, honestly*—just got hotter with age, while we women got grayer, softer, and needed a highlighter palette to fake our youthful glow.

"Sure, come in," I muttered with false gaiety, stepping back.

"Thank you." He moved past me, all clean pine and alpha male heat, and I tried not to inhale like a weirdo. "So, do you have a list of what was destroyed?"

"The display case on the left this time," I told him, keeping my voice steady while desperately not staring at the way his biceps flexed as he scribbled in his little black notebook. "We caught it early, so it didn't spread."

I was a fool to think he still thought of *us*.

I just missed my shot with him, I guessed.

Better that way—relationships just weren't my thing.

That was my story, and I was sticking to it.

Still, I wondered if maybe he ever thought about me. And yes, I hated that I wondered.

I handed him a list of the damage for the police report.

His fingers brushed mine, sending a stupid little shiver up my spine.

Do not make this personal, Bella.

He's just an attractive man you have history with.

No sparks. None. Zip. Nada.

"Are you alright, Bella?" His deep voice conjured butterflies in my stomach, and I closed my eyes for a moment just so my brain would have time to recalibrate.

"The damage is superficial—"

"I don't mean the bakery, Sugar. I mean you." His gaze softened, and damn it, my knees didn't need that. "It must be difficult being targeted."

"What do you mean? It's probably just some punk kids," I shrugged, trying for breezy.

"This is the second fire in a couple of months. Jaxson and I think it might be personal."

"Personal? But everyone loves me! I spread joy with cupcakes and donuts! Who would want to hurt me?"

The very idea I was being singled out made my stomach flip.

True, I'd considered it before. But having him say it aloud like that? Well, that just smarted.

"What do I do? Am I in danger?"

The question slipped out before I could stop it.

It wasn't like me to crumble in front of anyone, least of all Conrad Boman—Shifter deputy, ex-fling, and human embodiment of *handle with care*.

But when his big arms came around me in a solid, grounding hug, I didn't resist.

We were friends, right?

Sort of.

Just your average everyday consenting adult friends who'd slept together.

Twice.

Okay, three times if you counted that one night where neither of us actually slept.

And yeah, maybe I'd been the one to put the brakes on things, but some traitorous part of me had been quietly sulking that he'd stopped asking.

I mean, sure, it was my choice, but still *what if?*

Conrad was the kind of Shifter Witchy women whispered about—big, capable, steady, the kind who could lift you over his shoulder without breaking a sweat.

And I was sure plenty of women were willing.

Not that it was my business.

It wasn't. Totally not.

Tell yourself that, Bella.

Anyway, I had to admit, it felt really damn good to be close to him again.

"Hey, you're safe now," he murmured, holding me like he meant it.

The man was a world-class hugger—none of that stiff *pat-pat* nonsense.

He hugged with his whole body, warm and

protective, until the rest of the world kind of melted away.

"Lawd, I miss you, Sugar," he said softly, his Southern drawl coming out when I least expected it.

Conrad tipped my chin up with one finger, pinning me with his singularly focused green-eyed gaze.

Oh, no.

Oh, yes.

He leaned in slowly, giving me all the space in the world to step back.

I didn't.

I couldn't.

I needed that kiss.

Someone had been setting fires in my bakery.

My whole world was tilted.

But here, in his arms? I finally felt right again—*dangerously right.*

Like maybe everything would be fine if I just stayed right here.

So, maybe I wasn't as immune to Conrad Boman as I'd been telling myself all this time.

Maybe there were *things.*

Things he and I still needed to work out.

The problem was, I didn't have the time—*or the*

emotional bandwidth—to play twenty questions with my own heart right now.

My plate was full. And not in the fun, stacked-high-with-pastries way.

I had hang-ups, okay?

Deep, deep hang-ups.

Emotional scar tissue from relationships past, the kind that doesn't fade with a hot bath and a glass of wine.

Plus, I had the whole plus-size Witch thing. Which, in the supernatural world, was its own special brand of baggage.

We'd only just started seeing any recognition that we weren't *magically defective* just because we didn't fit into the sleek, slinky stereotype.

Meanwhile, every other supernatural species got their perfect physiques and freakish metabolisms handed to them on a glittery silver platter.

Werewolves could demolish an entire side of beef and still have abs you could grate cheese on.

Vampire women could eat their weight in molten chocolate cake and somehow only get shinier.

Even the freaking Selkies stayed slim—probably because they spent half their time swimming, but still.

And then, there was me.

Just your not-so-average Witch from New Jersey.

Calories loved me.

Worshiped me.

Practically built a temple in my honor and sacrificed their entire extended family straight to my hips, thighs, and soft belly.

I swear, my baked goods doubled in caloric value the second they got within a five-foot radius of my face.

And look, I'm not making excuses—*I own my curves.*

I earn them with the goods I bake. I dress them well. I am, objectively speaking, a whole damn snack in one woman-sized package.

But it's hard not to notice when everyone else can eat a dozen donuts—*a true baker's dozen*—and still look like they're ready for the supernatural swimsuit calendar, while I so much as look at a croissant and my jeans start plotting a mutiny.

But honestly—*honestly*—who in their right mind could resist a strawberry-dipped chocolate donut with rainbow sprinkles on just your average Wednesday?

Not this Witch.

Not ever.

And yes, that exact inability to say *no* to a baked

good also fed the entirely accurate—*though deeply annoying*—voice inside my head that liked to question Conrad's motives every time he came within a five-foot radius of me.

What's a guy like that doing with a Witch like you?

That snide little thought would slink in uninvited, setting up shop in my brain and making itself at home like it paid rent.

Because Conrad Boman wasn't just hot.

He was weaponized.

Tall, broad, chiseled like a Greek god who'd traded the toga for a Deputy's badge and biceps that could bench press my bakery's industrial ovens.

The man had hero written all over him, right down to the jawline that could cut glass.

Meanwhile, I was Bella Strega—curvy, cake-powered, and owner of the only bakery in Castor's Corner that could double as a crime scene thanks to recent firebug activity.

So yeah, you can see how the math didn't exactly add up in my head.

I had no idea what a guy like him saw when he looked at me—*and honestly?*

I wasn't sure I wanted to find out. Not if the answer was that I was just a *for now* kind of girl.

Especially with both my girls finding their happy endings with their mates.

Oh my Gaia, please no.

Not if I had to learn that he was only in it for the kicks, the giggles, and maybe a few late-night rolls in the sheets before moving on to someone with less frosting on her fingers.

Because here's the thing.

I'd already invested my heart.

I hadn't meant to. I'd tried so hard not to. But somewhere between his stupidly protective streak, the way he called me *Sugar* like it meant something, and the memory of how he kissed like sin itself, I'd gone and handed over pieces of myself I couldn't take back.

And I knew better.

Like my Nana always said, it's better to end things before they start—*less sweeping to do after the glass shatters.*

CHAPTER THREE-CONRAD

I SLOUCHED BACK in my chair at the Sheriff's office, spinning a pen between my fingers while staring at the stack of paperwork I had zero intention of finishing today.

My brain wasn't here—not even close.

It was about five blocks away, in a warm, sugary-smelling little bakery where the woman I wanted more than my next breath was probably up to her elbows in flour, frosting, and finding new and creative ways to avoid me.

Bella.

My Bella.

The only woman on Earth who could make a Python Shifter like me feel like an awkward teenager again.

She wasn't just beautiful—*though, Goddess help me, she was stunning*—she was *mine*.

My fated mate.

My other half.

My home.

Only she wouldn't admit it.

Her laugh haunted me.

Her scent—sweet sugar, vanilla extract, and rainbow sprinkles, plus a little something that reminded me of the moment before a summer storm—wrapped around my senses until my Snake wanted to coil up and never let her go.

The way her curves fit against me when I'd had the chance to hold her was burned into my memory like a brand.

And yet nothing.

Or rather, nothing more.

"For the Goddess' sake, Conrad, why don't you stop moaning and groaning and slither your ass down to The Tasty Tart and just mark that woman already?" Jaxson snapped, slamming his fingers against his keyboard.

"I tried! I mean, we already slept together," I moaned, dropping my head onto the desk like I was trying to fuse my skull with the wood. "She knows we fit. Hell, we're perfect together! I just can't figure out why she won't accept my claim."

Jaxson, lounging in the chair across from me like the smug mated Wolf that he was, smirked as he grabbed his mug of hot java. His gray eyes peered at me over the rim of his *#1 Sheriff* mug.

"Maybe she refused you because you're coming on like a battering ram instead of the perfect mate?"

Ryan, in the corner eating what had to be the biggest damn triple berry croissant in the entire state, let out a low chuckle.

"Yeah, you Python guys have this whole coil-'em-and-keep-'em instinct thing going, right? Maybe that's not exactly her style."

I sat up, glaring at both of them.

"You think I don't know that? I've been trying to go at her pace, but my inner beast is," I blew out a breath, shaking my head. "Let's just say, if it were up to him, Bella would already be claimed, marked, barefoot in my kitchen, and we'd be arguing about baby names."

Jaxson's grin widened.

"Sounds romantic. Try that. She'll love it."

"Shut up, Wolf," I grumbled, though one corner of my mouth twitched.

The truth was, I had been pacing myself.

Sort of.

For a guy like me, waiting a whole week after sleeping together was practically saint-level restraint.

But Bella? She was a wall—*gorgeous, soft, kiss-me-until-I-forget-my-own-name wall*—and she wasn't budging.

The thing was, I didn't just want her in my bed.

I wanted her in my life.

Waking up next to her.

Arguing about who left the coffeepot empty.

Dancing in the kitchen at midnight just because I could hold her close.

She was the one, the only one, and my snake knew it.

Now, I might not think much of Wolves and Bears, being a superior sort of Shifter myself, but let's face it—those guys got their mates to accept them.

So they had to be doing something right.

My beast shifted restlessly in the back of my mind, muscles coiling, ready to fight, to prove strength, to win her. But that wasn't going to work with Bella.

She wasn't prey.

She was the prize.

I shoved down all my hissing and growling and did what no self-respecting Python should ever have to do.

I begged.

"Please, guys. Help me out."

They smirked like I'd just handed them the winning lottery ticket.

Ryan set his gun down and leaned forward, elbows on his knees.

"First thing—stop chasing her like you're hunting dinner. Let her come to you."

"Exactly," Jaxson agreed. "And when she does, don't smother her. Give her space, but make sure she knows you're not going anywhere."

I narrowed my eyes.

"That's it? That's your big advice? Play dead and hope she trips over me?"

Jaxson shrugged.

"Worked for me."

Ryan grinned.

"Me too."

I groaned, leaning back in my chair.

"You two are impossible."

But the truth was, they'd answered.

As only real blood brothers could.

And maybe, possibly—*because really, I wasn't getting anywhere on my own and I only had everything to lose*—but just maybe, they were right.

Goddess, please be right.

CHAPTER FOUR-BELLA

A WEEK HAD PASSED since that tumultuous kiss with Conrad Boman.

And when I say *kiss*, I don't mean your average everyday smooch.

I mean the kind of kiss that could make a grown Witch reconsider her life choices, forget her own name, and possibly sign away her soul without reading the fine print.

He'd left with a resounding smack of his lips against mine.

The tease.

Ever since then, he'd been patrolling past my bakery most days, and I can only assume nights, too, when he was on duty as Deputy.

Oh, I told myself it was just a coincidence, that maybe The Tasty Tart just happened to be on the way to literally everything else in town.

But I wasn't buying my own excuses.

It was enough to make a Witch crazy.

My hormones were out of control, my concern over my mystery arsonist was gnawing at me, and I was cranky from lack of sleep.

And on top of all that? I was panting after a man I swore I wouldn't get serious about.

This was ridiculous.

I was the calm one.

The happy one.

The one who didn't need a man to make her day brighter.

The one who welcomed whatever excitement the new dawn brought, whether it was a delivery of perfect strawberries or a sudden frog rainstorm.

That was the beauty of my hometown.

Anything could happen at any given moment in Castor's Corner.

A supernatural population meant that expecting anything else was simply foolish.

I was rarely foolish.

Unless, of course, we were talking about my

experiences with men—*which, er, yeah, let's not unpack that just yet.*

Despite my best efforts, I'd been a confused mess these last few weeks.

And this was so *not* my norm.

Evie and Donny were usually the ones fretting about all the weird curveballs life threw us, while I reveled in them.

I'd always liked surprises.

Some of them were even good ones.

Take this morning, for example.

Surprise number one: Sunshine in the forecast after weeks of clouds and cold.

Nice surprise.

Surprise number two: When I pulled my hair into its usual ponytail, my freshly trimmed ends (thanks to Donny's magical scissors) bounced into soft curls all on their own.

Totally unexpected.

Totally cute.

Another win.

Surprise number three: I found a crumpled old scratch-off lottery ticket at the bottom of my Vera Bradley bag (one of my three hundred seventy-two, give or take). I scratched it off, and I won $4.

Hey, for a small business owner? That's practically a windfall.

So yeah, the day was shaping up nicely.

My magic was humming, my recipes for the Summer Solstice Festival were planned, and my besties were getting married at midnight on the big night.

I was baking their cake—*free of charge.*

Not because they couldn't afford to pay me (please, between Evie's inheritance and her mayoral salary and Jaxson's Sheriff-Wolf-whatever income, they were set), but because some things were too important to put a price tag on.

This was *my* gift.

From my hands, my magic, my heart, straight to theirs.

I was pulling out all the stops—tier upon tier of perfection, each layer more decadent than the last.

Hours of sketching, planning, and recipe testing had gone into this baby.

My kitchen table was buried under notes and swatches of fondant colors, little jars of edible shimmer, and enough cake boards to build a fort.

This wasn't just a cake.

Oh no. This was *the* cake.

The kind that made people gasp when they saw it and moan when they tasted it.

The kind that would be immortalized in wedding photos and whispered about at every future Summer Solstice Festival.

The kind that made Witches and Shifters alike weep frosting-induced tears of joy.

And it wasn't lost on me that I'd been waiting for this moment my whole life—my chance to create *the* quintessential wedding cake.

The one all other cakes would be measured against.

The fact it was for my two oldest and dearest friends?

That was just icing.

And honestly, the timing couldn't have been better.

Because I needed something—*anything*—to keep my brain from circling back to all things tall, sexy, and impossible to ignore.

Otherwise known as Conrad Boman.

The man was like the culinary equivalent of salted caramel.

Sweet, tempting, just the right amount of sinful, and absolutely impossible to get out of your head once you'd had a taste.

And thanks to that recent kiss—*you know what*

I'm talking about, uh huh, that kiss—I'd had more than a taste.

Which was exactly why I needed to keep my hands, my mind, and my heart busy.

So, if anyone asked, I wasn't avoiding my problems.

I was simply busy, elbow-deep in buttercream.

Sure, Bells, tell yourself that.

Anywho, the last few days had been quiet.

No suspicious smoke.

No mystery shadows lurking outside my shop.

No broken cutlery or upended trash cans.

I'd been lulled into a false sense of security, my mind wandering far too often to a certain tall, broad-shouldered, emerald-eyed—*ugh, no.*

Not going there.

Not out loud.

Things were looking up, and I was almost ninety-nine percent sure I was going to get over this little hiccup I was having in my brain—*not my heart*—over a certain sexy Python and emerge all the better for having refused his claim.

Right? Right.

It was just optimism galore in my neck of the woods, *er*, Castor's Corner.

That was my story, and yada yada, you know the drill.

The sky was still dark when I pulled my car into my designated space in The Tasty Tart's parking lot.

Something was amiss. The hair on the back of my neck started to rise. Petyr growled in his seat.

Oh no.

Sniff.

Oh no no no.

Sniff sniff.

Crap on a cracker!

"That's smoke, my Witchy," Petyr murmured from beside me.

"Oh no. Not again." My stomach dropped as I dialed 333—*our own Castor's Corner version of 911*—while already sprinting toward the back entrance.

I grabbed the fire extinguisher, whispered a quick enhancement charm, and blasted the storefront where a display rack was engulfed in flames.

"Stand back!" a deep voice ordered.

Conrad.

And right beside him—Ryan, Donny's mate, equally massive and equally heroic-looking in his firefighting regalia.

They took over without hesitation, but Petyr put

himself between me and the fire like the stubborn little puffball he was.

As my familiar, his entire job was to keep me safe, and he was very, very good at it.

"Outside, Bella. Now," Conrad commanded, stepping in front of me with his arms spread wide.

His face was grim, jaw tight, eyes locked on mine. Concern radiated from him in waves.

"He is right, come."

Petyr tugged me toward the curb.

I let him.

The last thing this magical town needed was me adding to the drama by inhaling smoke.

"You okay, my Witchy?" Petyr asked.

"Not really," I muttered, plopping down on the curb and pressing my hands to my face.

Normally, by now, the scent of fresh dough, sugar, and melted chocolate would be curling through my shop, drawing in customers like moths to a flame—*bad analogy, given the current situation, but still true.*

I lived for those early hours.

For kneading soft delicacies under my palms.

For working out my problems as I worked out the dough.

For filling trays with glossy pastries and wicked little

donuts stuffed with everything from cream cheese and lemon curd to chocolate ganache and bourbon caramel.

That was my magic. That was *me*.

And now, twice in a couple of months, someone had decided to take a match to it.

I had no idea why, but looking at the destruction that surrounded me, I had a terrible feeling things were going to get worse before they got better.

And I wasn't at all sure I could handle it.

CHAPTER FIVE—BELLA

SOME PEOPLE THOUGHT RUNNING your own business meant loads of free time and setting your own schedule.

Bless their sweet, clueless little hearts.

They couldn't be more wrong if they tried.

See, there was always something to be done. Inventory, invoices, bookkeeping, payroll—check, check, check, and ugh, so much more.

And it wasn't just the fact that these things needed doing.

Oh no. It was the fact that you—*the boss, the owner, the queen of all you surveyed*—were the one responsible for making sure they actually got done.

No magical paperwork Fairies.

No enchanted ledger that balanced itself overnight.

Just me, my coffee, my loyal staff—*I paid them very well, including all the sugary bonuses they could eat*—and my eternal to-do list that somehow grew longer every time I crossed something off.

Every morning—*and I mean pre-dawn morning, when the world is still dark and the only souls awake are Ghosts and Vampires headed home to their beds or coffins*—I was at the bakery, getting shizzle done.

Schedules didn't make themselves, you know.

Not anymore than my award-winning Double Chocolate Cupcake Bombs, which—*side note*—can double as real bombs if left out in the sun too long.

(*Long story. Don't ask. And definitely don't store them in your car in July.*)

It wasn't glamorous.

No one was filming me for a reality baking show as I hauled fifty-pound flour sacks or scrubbed frosting out of a mixing bowl the size of a hot tub.

And yet, I loved it.

Even the parts that made me want to hex my spreadsheet.

Because this was *my* bakery.
My passion.

My joy.

My thang.

My blood, sweat, tears, and real, old-fashioned buttercream went into every inch of it.

The moment I turned the key in the lock and stepped into that warm, yeasty air, the world made sense again—at least until someone tried to burn it down. *Twice.*

Which, for the record, made absolutely *no* sense.

Kinda like a certain Python Shifter's refusal to just fade gracefully into the background like an old Instagram trend.

I mean, honestly.

How's a Witch supposed to get over a guy if he keeps popping up everywhere like glitter after a crafting accident?

For fork's sake, give a girl some breathing room!

(Donny's been teaching me how to curse without actually cursing. Whaddya think? She says I'm at creative toddler level. And I'll take it.)

And all this while I'm in the middle of my ongoing experiments in the Holy Grail of Witchy baking.

Calorie-free goodies.

Yes, that's right.

Goodies that don't stick to your thighs, belly, or anywhere else Great Aunt Edna liked to pinch and comment on at family gatherings.

And I'm not talking about the *diet* kind where you pretend swapping sugar for something that tastes like powdered sadness is just as good.

No, I meant full-on, buttery, melt-in-your-mouth perfection that wouldn't add an inch to your hips, magically or otherwise.

When—*not if*—I cracked that code? My friends and I would be the happiest Witches in all of Castor's Corner.

Possibly the world.

There might be parades.

Definitely fireworks.

I was proud of my goodies.

And no, I didn't mean the ones I inherited from my awesome Italian and Viking ancestors—though, let's be real, those were top tier, too.

I was talking about my baked goodies, not my Witchy-metabolism-proof curves.

Still, credit where credit's due—*nobody filled out a triple D-cup like I did.*

I was basically the poster child for *hourglass, but with extra sand around the middle parts.*

The thing is, every other Witch in the known supernatural world seems to stay young and thin for hundreds of years.

The Goddess hands out eternal beauty like it's candy on Halloween.

And me? I got the longevity part, sure. At least, I'm assuming I did.

But the *magically maintain a size two without trying* gene?

Yeah, that one skipped me entirely.

It didn't matter how much I *watched what I ate*—and by *watched*, I meant actually gave in and tried starving myself that one time.

It was a disaster.

My magic went absolutely feral. I accidentally zapped my father right on his backside in the middle of Sunday dinner.

The man couldn't sit for a week.

Lesson learned.

Hangry Bella equals hazardous Bella.

Still—every other Witch in town could inhale a dozen donuts and not gain an ounce.

Take Magdelena, La Befana herself.

She's famous for hoovering half a dessert table without breaking a sweat.

She also loves my *Undeath By Chocolate* brownies

so much, she demands them at all her Coven gatherings.

I recently sent her two dozen as a thank-you for giving me Petyr, my familiar.

She replied that she had eaten them all in a single sitting.

And yet, still thin as a broomstick.

Meanwhile, I just look at a cookie, and my jeans get tighter.

Not that I hate my body—Goddess, no. I loved my curves.

But keeping them in check? That was a full-time job.

At least I didn't suffer alone. Donny and Evie were built the same—big bosoms, soft hips, the kind of bubble butts that made Shifters walk into lamp-posts, which was totally a perk by the way.

And we all shared the same appreciation for sweets. *Scratch that—addiction.* It was definitely an addiction.

Maybe it's in the blood.

After all, my besties and me? Well, it turns out we have more than our chunky butts in common.

Enter Grandpa Al—legendary Warlock, shameless flirt, and total hound.

Apparently, fidelity wasn't in his vocabulary.

Which, honestly, explained a lot, including why his Ghost was missing his magical no-no square (thanks, Evie's Nonna).

So there it was—proof positive.

Our *special* metabolism wasn't just a fluke of fate.

It was genetic.

The three of us weren't just besties, we were cousins. We shared the same bloodline. And sometimes?

Even the same jeans—*the denim kind.*

Made sense, right?

Anyway, it wasn't easy being part of the select few supernaturals who suffered from *tuchus giganta-mous*—an extremely rare and extremely stubborn condition passed down from my Aunt Edna's side of the family tree.

Thanks, Auntie. Really. Love the genes.

Of course, being a baker probably wasn't the wisest career choice if I wanted to slim down my, uh, *assets.*

But honestly? Of the three of us, I didn't have much of a problem with it.

I liked myself—hips, thighs, triple-Ds, and all.

The way I saw it, you can't spread joy with a side of insecurity.

Still, back to Petyr.

My familiar wasn't your average cute-and-cuddly magical sidekick. He was unusual, true, but his powers were ridiculously cool.

He didn't seem to have a limit to what he could do. I mean, where my Witchy magic had boundaries —*strict ones*—Petyr seemed to laugh at the very concept of rules.

My own magic? Kitchen magic. Domestic sorcery, as my Granny called it. Useful, yes, but not exactly flashy.

I couldn't stop time or levitate buildings or hurl fireballs at annoying people in line at the DMV.

My spells were confined to food, flavor, comfort.

They worked best in the kitchen, with my hands in the dough and my heart in the recipe.

Evie's magic was different—rare and wild.

She was a seer Witch, able to catch glimpses of past and future events like she was flipping through a cosmic photo album.

Donny's magic was closer to mine. She could see and mend inner hurts, weaving confidence into her clients' haircuts until they walked out of her salon taller, shinier, happier.

I guess of the two, I was more like Donny.

Our magic was about nourishment—hers of the spirit, mine of the stomach.

Not exactly earth-shattering, but it mattered.

Castor's Corner needed a baker, and I was the baker.

Easy peasy, right?

Only, not so much. Because if I was so valued, why was someone targeting me?

"I check on storage, my Witchy," Petyr told me before vanishing in that *blink-and-you-missed-it* way of his.

That little furball was faster than lightning when he wanted to be. Take the other day, I was moping in the kitchen, lamenting how much I missed my Granny's special banana extract, made from the now commercially extinct Gros Michel bananas.

I'd just muttered that I'd give anything for a taste of it again—poof!

Petyr disappeared for hours.

When he returned, not only did he have three bushels of perfectly ripe Gros Michels, but he was also sporting an Elvis-style pompadour and humming "Teddy Bear."

I still don't know where he went, and frankly, I'm a little afraid to ask.

Now I had a huge barrel of banana extract processing in my storeroom, right next to the walk-in fridge.

Once it was ready?

Oh, honey! I was going to bake a storm of banana nut loaves so good, they'd make angels weep.

It would also be the perfect time to test my next *guilt-free* recipe.

Trying to create a magical hack for weight loss was an ongoing thing. Donny, Evie, and I had long since accepted we'd probably always be the three curviest Witches in the county, but still a girl had to have goals. And I could still dream.

It would be nice not to gain ten pounds every time I got a craving for pineapple cheesecake, a giant chocolate-covered cannoli, or my vanilla cream Napoleons with fresh strawberries.

Yum.

See, I'd learned to bake at my grandmother's knee, perfecting her recipes before branching out into my own.

When I finally opened my shop, The Tasty Tart, it became an instant hit.

Not to brag (okay, maybe a little), but people lined up out the door for my pastries.

And now? My website and delivery business were booming.

People—*and by that I meant supes from around the world*—wanted my goodies.

But enough about all that.

Where was I?

Oh, right—Ryan packing up the firetruck, and Conrad stowing his gear before walking toward me.

Cue instant panic.

CHAPTER SIX-BELLA

I WAS STILL GLUED to the cold concrete curb outside my bakery, clutching the splintered remains of my favorite rolling pin.

The one Petyr had salvaged from beneath the charred wreckage of the ruined display rack.

I wasn't supposed to be sitting there answering questions about another mystery arson attack.

But my legs didn't feel like working, and my heart? Well, it was still somewhere between the shock of seeing flames in my bakery again and the way Conrad's jaw clenched every time he looked my way.

And neither of those things was making it easy to breathe.

I squared my shoulders and bit the inside of my

cheek. Time to put on my big girl pants and ignore the sexy Shifter while pretending my whole life wasn't in shambles.

I could do that.

Maybe. Kinda.

Oh, who was I forking kidding?

"I have to ask you some more questions, Bella."

I nodded for him to continue.

"So, you arrived here at 4:30 this morning?" Conrad asked, his voice that smooth, low rumble that made my insides do inconvenient things.

His expression was all business—grim, intent, those chiseled features sharpened by focus.

Which, frankly, was rude, because the man had no right to look that good while parts of my shop were still smoldering.

I tried not to admire him.

Really, I did.

But it was like telling myself not to breathe—it just wasn't happening.

He was damned gorgeous no matter what face he was making.

Ridiculous Witch.

Drooling over a man when your store is literally a crime scene.

Priorities, Bella.

"Yes, I got here about then," I mumbled, tucking a stray curl behind my ear and hoping I didn't look like I'd just rolled out of bed—*which, in my defense, I had.*

I still could not believe some jerk had started a fire in my bakery.

For. The. Second. Time.

I'd gone from irritated to suspicious to full-on homicidal about it.

"I think it's time we talked about who might have a grudge against you," he said.

Anger flared hot in my chest. "I'm part of the Witch Trifecta that keeps Castor's Corner safe," I snapped. "How could someone I know do this to me?"

"I'm not sure, Bella. Could you have a disgruntled customer? Someone who received a wrong order?"

"I do not get orders wrong!" I said, puffing up like a ticked-off hen. "My goodies are made with the best of intentions, and I fill each order precisely as it should be filled."

"Bella, I know you have a gift for baking. And for the record, I think your goodies are perfect," he rumbled in that deep, husky tone that wrapped around me like honey over warm bread.

And just like that, my bruised ego went from

sulking in the corner to humming happily in an apron.

I hated how much I liked the way he said it.

Don't be so needy, Bella.

"But if there's anyone with even the slightest grievance, it could help us," Conrad pressed gently.

Brave man, suggesting such a thing twice.

Pink and white sparks fizzed at my fingertips, and I quickly tucked my hands behind my back.

His eyebrow quirked up, but I only shrugged.

"I did use royal blue fondant on Grayson Fox's sixth birthday cake instead of cerulean blue, but that was only after checking with his mother," I admitted. "The cerulean dye was out of stock."

"Okay, that's a start."

"Fine. I ran out of Bavarian-filled donut holes for the library last Wednesday and substituted vanilla custard. And the senior center's order was late yesterday because my produce delivery was delayed."

He grinned—*actually grinned*—like I'd just told him the cutest joke instead of my most heinous professional crimes.

"Not sure any of those qualify as arson-worthy, but I'll look into it."

My heart gave a stupid little lurch.

The man was bewitching me, and he wasn't even a Wizard or Warlock.

It wasn't fair.

Out of the corner of my eye, I spotted Petyr by the dumpster, hauling trash.

"Sonovacockroach!" I yelped.

"What *isssss* it?" Conrad hissed, moving in front of me and scanning for danger.

"Is that my pink apron?" I asked my familiar.

"Sorry, my Witchy. It cannot be saved," Petyr said solemnly.

"Dammit!" I stomped my foot like a toddler denied dessert.

"Sorry about your apron, Maribella," Conrad murmured, the way he said my full name sent a ripple of heat through me that had nothing to do with the lingering smoke.

I was still clutching the broken remains of my favorite rolling pin, and between that and my apron, my emotions were riding the high-speed broom to Meltdown City.

"Maribella? Are you alright?" he asked, cautiously stepping closer.

That's when my magic decided to join the pity party.

Pink and white sparks shot from my fingers, and where they landed—*thunk*—hardtack appeared.

Not cookies.

Not croissants.

Hardtack.

The driest, blandest, most tooth-shattering edible ever conceived.

My magic only made it when I was truly, epically ticked off.

"Bella? Bella!" Conrad called my name, but I was already shouting into the early morning air.

"I don't know who you are, you loathsome, dirty, rotten arsonist! But I'm going to find you, and when I do, your goose is cooked!"

"Hey, it's gonna be alright now. Bella? You good?"

Conrad stepped over a pile of wretched crackers and gripped my shoulders, giving me a steadying shake.

His eyes—*those deep, mesmerizing pools of emeralds*—were full of worry.

That simmering smolder was doing things to me again, the kind of things that made me want to toss my good sense out the nearest window.

And for a second—*just a second*—I thought about letting myself fall into whatever this was between us.

But crunching sounds broke the moment.

I glanced down to see Petyr happily gnawing on a piece of hardtack like it was gourmet biscotti.

Not only that, but he'd invited Ivan and Gryn, who had materialized with their own bottles of vodka, to join in.

The three familiars were now sitting cross-legged on the pavement, playing *preferans* and snacking like they were at some kind of supernatural tailgate.

"Well, at least they'll eat through this before you open today," Conrad said dryly.

"Lucky me," I muttered, though I couldn't help noticing the way he was still standing close enough that I could feel his heat.

Too close for comfort.

Too close for a Witch trying to keep her heart safe.

And yet, I didn't step away.

CHAPTER SEVEN-CONRAD

AT THE TASTY *Tart*

"I have to ask you some questions, Bella. So, you arrived here at 4:30 this morning?"

I kept my tone neutral, professional, even though every nerve in my body was lit up like a live wire just being near her.

Her hair was pulled back, her cheeks pink from exertion—*or fury*—and the faint smell of sugar and smoke clung to her skin.

It was intoxicating, and not just because my Python was already convinced she was ours.

She nodded, lips tight. "Yes, I got here about then."

The more I questioned her, the more I could hear the frustration in her voice.

Hell, I felt it.

And it was killing me.

Another attempt to destroy her bakery in as many weeks, and each one had my inner beast coiling tighter and tighter around the need to protect her.

"I think it's time we talked about who might have a grudge against you," I said, already bracing for her reaction.

Her eyes flashed, that stubborn streak rising like the tide. "I'm part of the Witch Trifecta keeping Castor's Corner safe. How could someone I know do this to me?"

I didn't want to say it, but I needed to be thorough for her sake, asking her about the possibility of disgruntled customers and the like.

She puffed up instantly, arms crossing under her perfect, maddeningly distracting breasts.

I couldn't help the corners of my mouth curving as she told me off.

Sexy, badass, Witch. I see you.

"Bella, I know you have a gift for baking. And for the record, I think your goodies are perfect."

And I meant every damn word.

Her mouth softened just a little, and for a second, I thought I might've snuck past her defenses.

Then her chin came up again, stubborn as ever.

I kept right on with the questions, doing my duty as Deputy and possible mate.

And sweet Bella rattled off a few offenses—*the wrong shade of blue fondant, a substitution in donut filling, a late delivery*—and I had to bite back a laugh.

"Not sure any of those qualify as arson-worthy, but I'll look into it."

Her familiar darted past with something pink in his furry claws.

She spotted it first. The ruined remnants of her favorite pink apron.

Her face fell, and my chest tightened. But my Witch was no doormat. Almost as soon as it appeared, her sadness was replaced by something else.

Anger.

Determination.

A promise for vengeance.

And I couldn't have been prouder of her.

But before I could say anything, her magic flared—*pink and white sparks shooting from her fingertips*—and suddenly we were ankle-deep in hardtack.

"Bella?" I tried, stepping closer, but she was in full Witch fury, shouting at the unknown arsonist like she could will them into submission.

I put my hands on her shoulders and gave her a firm, steadying shake.

"Bella? Bella!"

"I don't know who you are, you loathsome, dirty, rotten arsonist! But I'm going to find you, and when I do, your goose is cooked!" She shouted, breasts heaving with exertion, and pig that I was, I looked.

Hell yes, I looked.

"Hey, it's gonna be alright now. Bella? You good?"

Her eyes met mine, and for a beat, I felt that pull again—the one that made me want to scrap every professional boundary and just claim her here and now.

My beast hissed, pushing for it.

But this wasn't the time.

Instead, I kept my voice even, my grip gentle, and willed her to take that breath.

"I'll be back to check on you later."

"Just go. I'm fine," she grumbled.

But I could see behind the lie.

This really shook her.

And to me, that was unforgivable. In fact, it made me furious.

"Bella, I promise you, I am going to do everything in my power to make sure you're safe."

Big blue eyes peered into mine, and with a subtle dip of her chin, she dismissed me.

I didn't want to go, but there was nothing more I could offer her at that moment.

Feelings of failure and the need for revenge clawed at me, but I had a report to file.

When I turned my head, Petyr nodded at me, and I knew the Domovyk was telling me without words that he'd guard my sweet Bella in my absence, and I believed him.

It was the only way my beast would let me leave.

Later–Mayor's Office

Jaxson was leaning against the corner of Evie's desk, arms crossed, wearing his Sheriff face. Evie was behind it, flipping through paperwork but looking entirely too amused for the topic at hand.

"Another attempt was made on the bakery this morning," I reported. "I'm requesting clearance to keep watch—*round the clock*—until we catch whoever's doing this."

"Is she okay?" Evie's head snapped up, and Jaxson placed a large hand on her shoulder, offering his comfort to his mate.

Something I wished I had the right to do to mine. But I had to sit on those feelings for now.

But hopefully not for much longer.

"Yes, Bella is fine. She wasn't hurt," I said, and Jaxson nodded, all business.

Evie exhaled, and it warmed me to know how much she cared about Bella. I mean, I knew they were close—*her, Donny, and Bella*—but my sweet Witch always struck me as a bit of a loner. It was as if she purposely set herself apart.

Like she didn't seem to understand she was every bit as valuable, important, and powerful as her two best friends.

I wanted to correct that. To make sure she knew just how amazing she was. If only she would let me.

"Makes sense to me. She's part of the Trifecta, and if someone's targeting her, it could be about more than just the bakery. I'll tell Ryan to keep an extra eye on Donny, too." Jaxson's growly voice interrupted my thoughts, and I nodded my understanding and agreement.

Evie tilted her head, eyes narrowing with an impish gleam.

"Are you sure you're not just trying to get in Bella's pants?"

"What? No, I—" I started, heat creeping up my neck.

"Well, why the heck not?"

"Wait. What?"

"I approve!" she announced before I could dig my hole any deeper. "My bestie might be gun-shy about *ye old badoinkadoinking,* but if you feel about her the way my man feels about me, I don't see the problem. Woo her, dammit! Witches need to be wooed!"

I blinked, trying for professionalism.

"Um, I'm here to talk about an official protection detail, Mayor Castor."

She waved a dismissive hand.

"Mm hm. And if some romantic gestures happen to coincide with the official protection? Well, that's just efficiency, Deputy."

Jaxson's mouth twitched, clearly enjoying my discomfort.

"Sounds like you've got your marching orders, Conrad," Jaxson said with way too much satisfaction. "Keep Bella safe—and apparently bring flowers."

"Uh, yes, sir?"

Yeah, it came out like a question, which only made Evie's smirk wider.

Look, the last thing I needed was to have my complete and utter failure at wooing my mate dissected in front of *Castor's Corner's* golden couple.

For fuck's sake, a man could only take so much.

I was this close to asking if they wanted to critique my kissing technique while we were at it.

But when the mayor and the sheriff—*who also happened to be your boss*—gave you orders, you didn't argue.

You nodded, you smiled, and you prayed you'd live to regret it later.

At any rate, my Python was already fully on board with both objectives.

He heard *keep her safe* and *bring gifts* and immediately started planning our mating ceremony.

I was just hoping to survive the courtship phase first.

CHAPTER EIGHT-BELLA

AFTER CONRAD LEFT, it was all I could do to pick up the pieces—*literally*—and move on.

Hardtack still littered the sidewalk in sad, stale mounds, but the three Domovyks were having the time of their lives.

They'd turned cleanup into a vodka-fueled snack fest, chomping through the vile stuff like Evie and I went through strawberry custard donut holes after wine night.

Petyr suddenly jumped up, ears twitching, and shouted something in his native tongue—a language that sounded like Russian, Romanian, and Klingon had all gotten drunk together and decided to raise a baby.

I didn't have a clue what he said.

But judging from the vein pulsing in his furry little forehead, it wasn't "Hey, let's all hug it out."

Petyr was generally my happy-go-lucky kitchen shadow, but ever since we'd been targeted by some pyro-happy punk, his typically cheerful magical panties had gotten into a gnarly twist.

I couldn't blame him.

He'd been cleaning up more fire damage than frosting lately, and even a magical being had a burnout point.

That he was still doing it for me made tears sting my eyes.

"My Witchy must not cry!" Petyr puffed out his chest like a tiny, homicidal general. "The arson must be stopped, da? I will set trap for him and tear him limb from limb!"

"Oh, um, catching them would be nice. But maybe no limb-tearing?"

"Fine. Will make torture device instead, da?"

Yikes. I made a mental note to set up a Swoosh call with Magdelena—she spoke at least fourteen magical languages and was great at talking familiars down from murder.

But that could wait.

Right now, I had a whole laundry list of things to do.

1. *Finish cleaning up this mess before the smell of burned sheetrock, lighter fluid, and my singed pride made me faint.*
2. *Give my statement to a certain tall, devastatingly sexy firefighter-slash-deputy who I'd been avoiding ever since we slept together and I snuck out the next morning without so much as a "later, gator."*
3. *Get the bakery up and running before a line of caffeine-deprived, sugar-hungry supernaturals decided to stage a coup.*

The Tasty Tart was *the* morning spot in Castor's Corner, and people here were creatures of habit.

Once, I came back from vacation a day late and found actual picketers outside my door.

It was traumatic—*for them and for me.*

So I tied on a fresh apron—not my favorite, pink one, but it would have to do—and I swept, scrubbed, and polished like my life depended on it.

The damage could have been worse—even I was big enough to admit that.

It was mostly on one side of the storefront. Of

course, some things took bigger hits than others. Like one of my custom floor-to-ceiling oak racks, and a patch of wall behind it.

But still, *wood was good.*

That was becoming my motto now.

"Put it on a business card," I muttered, kicking at a splinter.

Right after I finished sweeping, I fumigated with a tried-and-true little hex I learned from my mother —*who invented it the day she'd had quite enough of Dad's post–taco night air raids*—I planted my feet, raised my hands, and chanted:

"By thyme and sage, by lemon bright,
Purge this place of stink and blight.
From floor to rafter, cleanse the air,
Leave sweetness, warmth, and love to spare.
Goddess bless my humble shop —
and please, no more eau de gym sock!"

The magic swirled, sparkled, and whisked away every trace of burned sheetrock, lighter fluid, and bad memories until my bakery smelled like fresh lemon cake again.

Once it was over, I stood basking in the glow of my accomplishments until I noticed the brand new, state-of-the-art magical alarm system above the door blinking at me.

So, I gave it the finger.

The alarm hadn't stopped *anything*.

Our mystery firebug had waltzed right past it, torched my shelf, and destroyed several of my favorite things—my pink apron, my rolling pin, my award placard, and the mug Evie and Donny gave me with all three of us grinning like idiots.

Who did that, anyway? Who went out of their way to destroy personal items in a place of business? And why, for fork's sake?

"Bella?"

I was still mulling when a deep voice spoke right behind me.

"Aghhhh!" I yelped, jumping so hard my magic shot out in a burst of pink-and-white glitter that materialized into—*yep*—more hardtack.

Conrad froze mid-step, hands raised.

"Sorry for scaring you, Sugar—uh, Maribella."

Sugar? Goddess, help me.

My heart did a full triple axel.

Why was he back?

Wasn't it bad enough he'd already fried my brain earlier with that smoldery concern and big, protective presence?

"Um, someone called about some noise," he said, stepping closer, "and I decided to check before I went off shift, make sure you were alright. Are you?"

"Am I what?" I asked, because apparently my brain had exited the building.

"Are you alright?" he repeated softly, like it mattered to him in a way that made my chest ache.

He was close enough now that I caught the faint scent of smoke, cedar, and something darkly warm that was all Conrad.

My traitorous eyes tracked the line of his jaw, the curve of his mouth.

My magic hummed under my skin, desperate to close the distance.

I pressed my lips together before I did something truly stupid.

Like grab his shirt, drag him against me, and give the entire street a live demonstration of why Witches and Pythons were a combustible combination.

My heart was practically pounding out of my chest at Conrad's sudden appearance.

And really, was it *legal* for a man to look that good when half my bakery still looked like a crime scene and my hair was doing a frizzy halo impersonation?

"Bella? I needed to check on you myself before I

went off shift after that noise complaint. So, are you okay, Sugar?"

"Huh?" I asked brilliantly, because apparently coherent thought was no longer my thing.

He smiled slowly then, and he stepped closer.

He was all broad shoulders and infuriatingly calm male confidence.

And I was hard-pressed not to melt into a puddle of goo at his boot-clad feet.

I pressed my thighs together, trying not to imagine how good he kissed, and did other *things*.

Hell, I was hanging on by a thread here, people.

Seconds away from giving the magical surveillance cameras a real show.

Yowza.

"You work fast," he said, scanning the shop with his cop eyes.

I followed his gaze, feelings of pride filling me.

I mean, how often did a man notice when a woman worked hard?

Not many if Granny was to be believed.

"I suppose, but that's mostly because of Petyr."

"Petyr, huh? Are you and your familiar having any issues? I noticed he was a little *possessssive* of you earlier," he added with a slightly growly hiss.

Ermagerd.

Just like that, lust sucker-punched me right in the gut. Conrad Boman had the sexiest, huskiest voice I had ever heard.

That snaky hiss at the end of words that didn't even end in an S?

Yeah, my panties were waving a white flag and begging for mercy.

"No, Petyr and I get along great. In fact, he's so happy here, he's about to ask Magdelena if he can bring his wife and sons over."

"Oh. I didn't realize he was married," Conrad replied. "That's good. What about you?"

"What about me what?"

"Any ex-boyfriends with grudges? Someone who would want to hurt you, Bella?"

I frowned.

Sure, I had exes—men I'd dated, kissed, baked for—but only one who'd broken my heart, and he'd moved to Chicago years ago.

"Um, I don't think I should discuss that with you," I mumbled.

"It's to keep you safe," he insisted, but something about the whole thing made me antsy.

"Fine, but the only ex I have who might want to cause me grief is Jameson Vorhees, but he took a position with the Warlock World Coven and moved to Chicago."

"Vorhees," he growled, jotting the name down like he was adding it to his personal hit list. "Anyone else?"

"Uh, no. You alright there?"

"Sorry, I might be feeling a little *possessssive* of you myself," he confessed, and his eyes, oh my Goddess, his eyes were glowing.

Whether it was lust or jealousy, I couldn't say.

But either way, the man was smoking hot.

"No reason for you to be," I hedged.

"Isn't there, Sugar? I know how you look when you're rounding that bend to ecstasy. I know what you taste like at three o'clock in the morning. I know those desperate little sounds you make when you like the things I do to your body. So yeah, I'd say there's plenty of reasons for me to covet you, sweet Witch," he murmured, his voice wrapping around me like molten chocolate.

And I know I shouldn't, but I liked it. A lot.

"That's in the past," I said, but my voice cracked, and even I didn't believe me.

Faker.

"You know I can hear lies, don't you, Sugar? Those memories of you and me together? They've been playing over and over in my head since that night."

"So what difference does it make? We slept together. It was a one-off."

"Not for me. Never for me. I still want you, Maribella Strega. All the time. And I promise you, little Witch, I'm not giving up."

"No?" I tilted my chin, pretending I wasn't already half-melting from the heat in his voice. "You say that, Conrad, but you will. You'll get bored. Find something else shiny to chase."

His eyes locked on mine, molten and unblinking.

"Nuh uh. No way. No how. I'm not going anywhere. And when you're ready to finally admit you want me, too? I'll be right here. Waiting for you."

It should've sounded cocky.

Instead, it slid under my skin like warm honey, coating every raw, vulnerable part of me I kept carefully walled off.

With a handful of words, the man had my heart pounding like I'd sprinted up three flights of stairs and my magic sparking like I'd just mainlined espresso and sugar.

I shut my eyes, desperate to hide the truth—that every nerve ending I owned was leaning toward him, hungry for more.

But wanting Conrad Boman was dangerous.

The kind of dangerous that left you raw and bleeding when it ended.

He was lethal, not because of his strength or the fact that he could probably coil around me and squeeze the breath right out of my lungs, but because he could get into places no one had ever been.

The private places.

The ones I didn't let anyone touch.

Dude—get your mind out of the gutter! I was talking about emotional places, for Pete's sake.

I mean, he'd already touched everywhere else, if I was being honest.

Still, falling for him would be emotional suicide, and I'd survived that once before. I wasn't dumb enough to sign up for a repeat performance.

At least, that's what I told myself.

Only my foolish, traitorous heart clearly hadn't gotten the memo.

It thudded against my ribs, reckless and eager, whispering lies about *happily ever afters* and forever matebonds.

It wanted to believe him.

It wanted my brain to shut up and just let it happen.

But I couldn't afford to fall for that line.

Not again.

Not with him.

If I did and it all went bad? Something told me I'd never recover.

Maybe I was too big a coward for my own good.

But whoever said it was better to have loved and lost was a masochist, that much I was sure of.

At least, I used to be.

CHAPTER NINE-CONRAD

SHE TRIED to brush me off with a quiet, defiant little whisper.

"You just want what you can't have. It's the chase you crave. It'll pass."

I almost laughed.

Pass?

Like hell it would.

She eased back a step, putting space between us like she thought distance could change anything.

Cute.

The problem was, space didn't work on me.

Not with her.

Every inch she gave me just made my Python coil tighter, already planning how to close it.

She didn't get it.

This wasn't a crush.

It wasn't some shiny-object phase I'd move on from.

Bella Strega had wrapped herself around my ribs from the first bite of her damn chocolate cream pie, and she hadn't let go since.

"I told you already, but I'll repeat it however many times you need to hear it, sweet Witch. This thing between us? It isn't gonna pass. It's not something I'll get over, like chicken pox," I told her, voice low and steady so she knew I meant every word.

"Conrad—"

"You had your say, Sugar, and I hate to interrupt, but I believe you need to hear this again. So, let me say it, okay?"

She nodded. Those blue eyes of her were so big, so crystal clear, I was liable to drown in them.

Oddly enough, that was more than okay with me.

"I'm not going anywhere. Got it? You just let me know when you're ready for me. I'll be right here, Bella. Waiting. Watching. Praying for the day you're ready to accept my claim."

The way her pupils blew wide at that—*yeah, she felt it, even if she didn't want to admit it.*

I felt it, too.

All the way down to my bones.

The sound she made—*soft, breathy, and unguarded*—shot through me like a live wire.

My restraint frayed.

I bent, catching her mouth with mine in a kiss that wasn't polite or patient.

I kissed her like she was already mine—because she was, whether she'd accepted it yet or not.

And, fuck, yes.

She kissed me back.

Oh, damn, she *kissed me back*.

Sweet Goddess, the way her lips moved with mine, the way her fingers curled like she was fighting the urge to grab me and hold on—it was enough to make a man forget his own name.

When I finally forced myself to pull away, she swayed, and my hands tightened around her waist, keeping her upright. I couldn't help the grin that slid across my mouth.

"Careful, Sugar," I murmured, my voice still rough from kissing her. "Wouldn't want you falling for me."

She shot me a glare that didn't match the flush in her cheeks.

Which was exactly when I noticed a streak of flour smudged high on her cheekbone.

I don't know what possessed me, but I reached

up—*slow, deliberate*—and brushed my thumb along her skin.

I felt the warmth of her cheek under my hand, heard the sharp hitch in her breath when my fingers lingered just a second too long.

"Missed a spot," I said, my voice pitched low enough it barely carried.

I licked the flour off my finger, moaning at her soft flavors still clinging to it.

Her eyes locked on mine, and for one tight, suspended moment, the world outside that bakery didn't exist.

Yeah. She could keep telling herself I'd get bored.

That I'd walk away.

But we both knew the truth.

I wasn't going anywhere.

That sweet Witch was all mine.

And more so? I was hers.

Every single inch of me belonged to her.

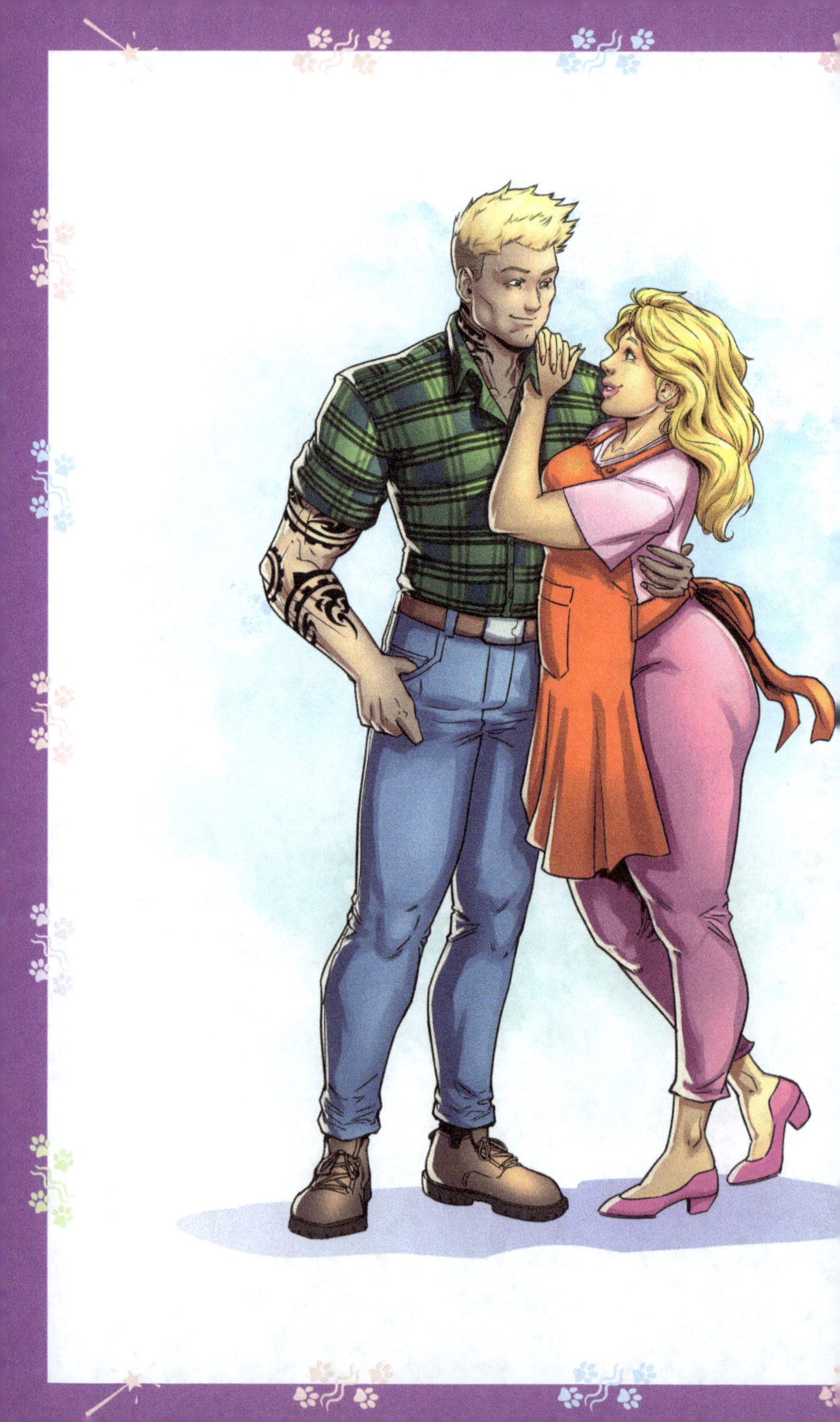

CHAPTER TEN-BELLA

LATER THAT WEEK

I'D BEEN fire-free for a few days, and that should've been cause for celebration.

No scorched walls.

No smoldering racks.

No Deputy Boman darkening my doorway with his broad shoulders, his deep voice, his unfairly green eyes—*ugh.*

This was the problem.

No Deputy Boman.

I didn't know what game he was playing, but maybe I'd been right all along.

Maybe he'd found something shiny to chase—*like a taller, skinnier Witch who didn't smell faintly of powdered sugar and vanilla bean 24/7.*

My heart stuttered and I swear I saw sad face emojis swirling around in my brain.

My Witch-proof smart phone chirped, and I looked down at a message from Donny.

She'd been sending me pics of bridesmaid dresses for days now and I had to say—I hated all of them.

Okay, that wasn't fair.

I mean, I was feeling lousy, but it wasn't Donny's fault.

Of course, it could be the fault of her bombing me with images of what amounted to miles and miles of chiffon, lace, and, ugh, taffeta in every color under the sun.

The truth was, maybe—*maybe*—I was a little frustrated.

A little sexually frustrated.

Not even my best vibey was taking the edge off, and that sucked.

So much so, I'd been toying with the idea of letting a certain snaky Deputy's charms to work next time I saw him—only, I haven't seen him!

So yeah, maybe I'd been cutting off my nose to spite my face by keeping Conrad at arm's length.

Not literally, of course.

My nose is adorable and would look weird in a jar.

But my metaphorical *nose*?

Oh yeah, I'd hacked that baby clean off with a serrated bread knife.

Because here's the truth.

I wanted him.

I wanted him in that hopeless, inconvenient, wake-up-at-3AM-thinking-about-his-stupid-hands way.

And he seemed *fine* without me.

Which was so rude, by the way.

Business, at least, was good.

I'd been elbow-deep in fondant all afternoon, working on improvements to the wedding cake design for Evie and Donny, and I couldn't wait to unveil it at our monthly bonfire.

It was going to be a showstopper—nine tiers, sugared roses, gold leaf accents. The kind of cake that made angels weep and diabetics panic.

I just had to lock up and reset the alarm before I left.

"Good evening, Bella!" a shrill voice rang out, and I cringed.

Why did this always happen?

Mrs. Gennaro, a longtime customer, breezed into the bakery just as I was literally—literally—reaching to flip the window sign from OPEN to CLOSED.

I inhaled a fortifying breath, determined not to let my inner gremlin show.

But really?

It was 5:59. I closed at 6:00.

"Hello, Mrs. Gennaro," I said, pasting on my professional smile as she tottered her petite self to the counter.

Normally, I had at least one other person working the front at closing time, but my new part-timer, Mira, had to leave early today for "Witchy goat familiar yoga" (don't ask).

So I'd been juggling the ovens, the register, and the mail orders all by my lonesome for the last two hours.

I'd sent the rest of my crew home already, because—logic.

But here I was, about to become a cautionary tale in Retail 101.

If you're here, you're open.

That was one of Granny's golden rules, and the voice in my head sounded exactly like her when I thought it.

And she was right, dang it.

I was here.

So I was open.

Even if my feet ached, my hair smelled faintly of

buttercream, and I could no longer feel my left pinky toe.

Petyr would be back any second.

He'd gone to my house to grab the half gallon of paint I'd left in the garage so we could finally finish repairing the wall the arsonist had torched.

We'd patched it days ago with spackle, but thanks to the week-long rain, it had taken forever to dry.

I know what you're thinking.

Why not use magic?

Well, magic came with rules.

And one of those was the big, murky, "no personal gain" clause that could and would bite you in the butt if you weren't careful.

So, elbow grease it was.

Paint, a little sweat equity, and a new baker's rack from Happy's Natural Wood Furniture & Lumber.

That Beaver Shifter could build a shelving unit that belonged in a fairy tale.

By tomorrow, you'd never know my shop had been the target of a pyro's idea of a fun night out.

Speaking of which, you little creep. Wait till I find you.

I heard the back door creak and Petyr's distinctive muttering as he came in, no doubt grumbling about the "paint for my Witchy" like it was a royal decree from the Tsar himself.

That little Domovyk was more protective of me than a guard Dragon, and if I let him off his leash, I was ninety-nine percent sure he'd string our mystery arsonist up in the town square.

Petyr was a good familiar.

Loyal, grumpy in a charming way, and the best moral support a girl could ask for.

He made me want to be a better Witch—and after this week, I was absolutely baking him something special as a thank-you.

But first, I had to survive Mrs. Gennaro.

Then, I had to make it to our monthly bonfire, drink something hot and alcoholic, and while I was readying myself, I had to try really hard not to wonder if a certain Python Shifter would be there.

Easy peasy, lemon squeezy.

Or it would be if Mrs. Gennaro hurried up.

CHAPTER ELEVEN—BELLA

THIRTY-NINE MINUTES *Later*

I stood there like the world's most patient shop-keeper (*read: lying through my teeth*) while the old biddy peered into my display case, squinting as though the last remaining tray of day-old biscotti might suddenly reveal the mysteries of the universe.

Spoiler: they would not.

Half the shelves were bare—*I'd already started clearing things away for tomorrow*—but there she was, humming and leaning in like the fate of Castor's Corner rested on whether she went with a cinnamon scone or a sugar cookie.

Lady, I had things to do.

A wall to paint, for one.

And after that? Haul my curvy Witch butt out to the pine barrens for our monthly Trifecta gathering.

That's right. It was that time again.

And no, not that time of the month—our collective hormones were none of your business.

I was talking Trifecta time.

Every month, like clockwork, my cousins-slash-besties-slash-fellow-hot-Witches and I hiked out to our little hidden clearing deep in the forest—*right on top of some serious ley lines*—to give the wards around our town a magical tune-up.

There was always a bonfire.

There was always singing, chanting, and communing with the Goddess.

And yes, there was always some enthusiastic naked dancing under the moonlight—because nothing says *protective barrier magic* quite like three buxom Witches shaking what their ancestors gave them in the flicker of open flame.

You think I'm kidding.

I am not kidding.

It kept Castor's Corner safe from mortal eyes.

Which was important.

The last thing we needed was a tour bus full of non-magicals rolling into town and Instagramming their way through our secrets.

And sure, a few Shifters had slipped through over the years.

Not our fault.

Mostly.

To be fair, Jaxson made an excellent Sheriff. Ryan was a great Fire Chief and in my kitchen, he was magic. And Conrad—*ugh.*

Conrad was making a name for himself as both a Deputy, a firefighter, and an electrician, and I was thrilled for him.

Really.

Couldn't be happier.

Also, I really hated the way we'd left things.

Because Conrad was confusing.

One second, he was all heat and smoldering snaky kisses.

The next, he was cool enough to chill the butter in my mixing bowls.

He turned on and off faster than my set of magical mixing bowls.

I mean the man kissed me like I was his last meal, then poof! He vanished for days.

And me? I was right to say no.

I simply wasn't built for that kind of emotional roller coaster.

Why couldn't the man just be happy with a little

no-strings boinking?

Was that so unreasonable?

The fact was relationships and I, well, let's just say we'd never been on speaking terms for long.

The second I agreed to be someone's girlfriend, the diet books would mysteriously start appearing, followed by lectures about *healthy lifestyle choices* and *necessary self-improvement.*

Newsflash, boys, I liked myself just fine.

Also, fork off.

I mean, yes, I had Monday-through-Sunday underwear, but that's called being organized.

And yes, my Monday panties said *Bakery Girl Forevah* on them, but that wasn't just laundry—*it was a lifestyle.*

Even pudgy, I was cute as hell.

And if a man couldn't appreciate that? Well, I had an entire drawer full of battery-operated optimism.

Sure, sex with an actual person was better, but it also came with things like feelings and the possibility of heartbreak.

And I wasn't interested in falling into that trap just because one six-and-a-half-foot-tall Python Shifter could kiss me into next week.

Which brought me back to the current problem: I

still needed to get Mrs. Gennaro out the door before I was late to the bonfire.

Donny and Evie were counting on me, and the former might take it as a personal betrayal if I showed up after moonrise, jeopardizing their joint wedding.

See, if the wards weren't reinforced then Castor's Corner was likely to get hit by some horribly inconvenient force—magical or otherwise.

And no one wanted that on any average day, never mind, with two of the town's Witch Trifecta's nuptials coming up.

"Mrs. Gennaro, have you decided what you'd like?" I asked, inching toward polite-but-firm territory.

"What, dear?" she said, blinking up at me like I'd just spoken in Parseltongue.

"I said, what can I help you with?"

"Oh, well," she sighed and looked around at the mostly empty shelves. "Everything goods been put away. Am I really late again?"

"In fact, I was just about to close—"

"Well, I'm glad I caught you then! The Castor's Corner Charmed Embers Women and Witches Social Club is having a special meeting tonight."

"That's nice," I said through my customer-service smile.

"Yes, and we're not just doting Grannies talking knitting patterns, oh no. We have important issues to discuss."

"I see. So, how can I help you?"

"As Vice President, I said I'd get the goodies for tonight's emergency meeting. Don't you want to know what it's about?"

She paused for dramatic effect.

My eyes flicked to the clock.

Tick tock, tick tock.

"Um, sure. Why not?"

"Well, Mr. Dorian is at it again, accusing someone's pet of eating his zinnias and prize marigolds. Can you believe the nerve? Downright insulted us, he did—accused us of being bad pet owners!"

"Oh my," I said, already picturing Donny's face when I showed up late and covered in powdered sugar.

Because clearly, the Goddess was testing me tonight.

Tick tock. Tick tock.

"So, we are starting a neighborhood watch and we are gonna find whose little furry bundle is up to no good," Mrs. Gennaro said, nodding with the gravitas of someone announcing the capture of an international jewel thief.

"I see. Well, that is fascinating. Sounds like hungry work. How about I put together a variety box just for you gals?" I offered, pasting on my biggest please-take-the-hint-and-go smile.

"Oh, I don't know. I might take my time and look around," she hedged, tapping her long fingernails on the counter in an almost slow-motion taunt.

I knew that look.

She was stalling.

Typically, when one of the older customers wanted to linger and chat, I obliged.

I mean, I liked being the friendly neighborhood baker-slash-listener-slash-keeper-of-town-gossip.

But tonight? Nope.

Not an option.

I had things to do.

Magic to cast.

Cousins to meet.

Wards to strengthen.

And possibly a small emotional crisis to continue having over a certain infuriatingly sexy deputy, but that was my business.

"I'll do it for half price," I blurted, instantly regretting it.

My voice came out like I was announcing a Black Friday sale, not desperately trying to make my customer choose a cookie and move along.

Her eyes lit up. "Deal!"

Well, I'd just been played. Again.

I hurried around the counter to grab one of my multicolored pastry boxes while Mrs. Gennaro watched with a predatory gleam in her eyes.

The woman was a sly old fox—not literally.

Literally, she was half Witch, half Ostrich Shifter.

That explained her knobby knees, ridiculously long neck, and tendency to stare at people like she was assessing whether they were worth pecking.

Her great-great-grandfather had immigrated to Castor's Corner from Australia after WWI, bringing his unique Shifter genes with him.

Honestly, it made her sort of cool.

Well, when she wasn't single-handedly making me late.

"Here you go," I said, tying the string into a neat bow.

I took her cash, thanked her, and herded her out the door like a one-woman ostrich wrangler.

The moment she was out, I flipped the sign to CLOSED with a flourish.

Then I turned toward the back. "Petyr! Got the paint?"

The door creaked open, and my familiar shuffled in, his little claws clicking against the tile.

Petyr was not your average Witch familiar.

No bat, owl, cat or talking zebra, like the one Mrs. O'Reilly kept in a stable in her backyard,

Oh no. Not for me or my girls.

Domovyks were their own category of supernatural—super strong, ridiculously loyal, magically gifted, and entirely incapable of blending into polite society.

Where most familiars were decidedly normal, Petyr was well, imagine a three-and-a-half-foot-tall furball with shaggy gray-and-black hair, bulbous eyes, curled ram-like horns, and a tail that dragged like he was sweeping the floor everywhere he went.

Add a dash of Slavic house-spirit mythos and the attitude of a retired mob boss, and that was my Petyr.

Goddess, help me.

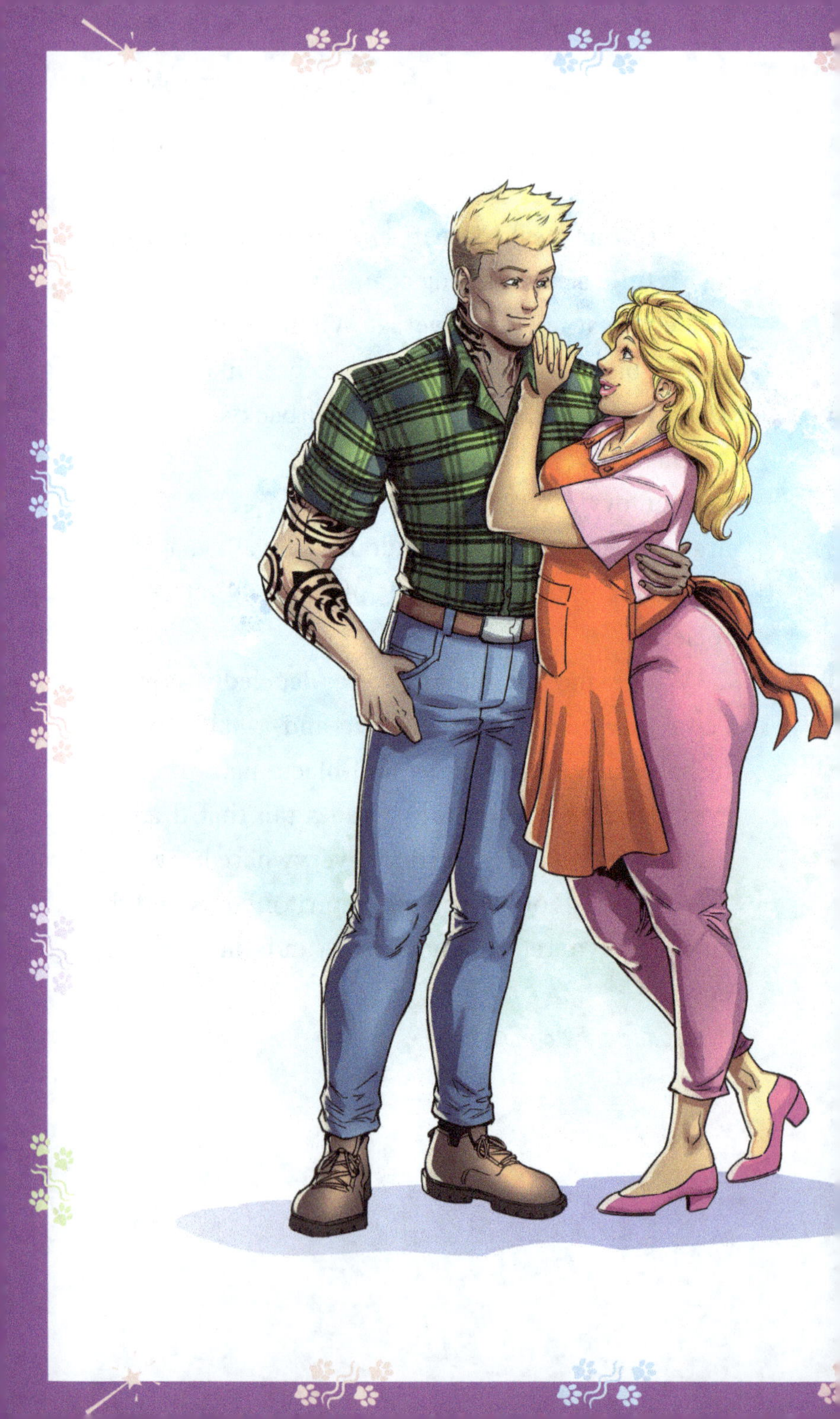

CHAPTER TWELVE-BELLA

"YES, my Witchy. I got the paint. You have enough Totally Teal in satin finish to fix the spot," he said, setting the can down like it was a sacred offering.

Then, muttering under his breath, "I don't see why I could not fix for you."

"It'll upset the balance if I let you use too much magic in here, Petyr. You know that," I reminded him, for the thirty-seventh time this month.

"But I wish to help."

"I know you do, but when you signed on to be my familiar, you agreed to protect, serve, and help me grow my abilities. You can't do that if you just do everything for me," I said, giving him my best stern-older-cousin voice.

"Yes, but Bella, you must let me help tonight."

"You are helping," I pointed out. "Who went back to the house for the paint?"

"Me," he admitted, plopping his furry butt onto my clean countertop and crossing his legs like he was settling in for a fireside chat.

Yeah. Definitely wiping that counter down before baking tomorrow.

When Petyr worked in the kitchen, he wore a tiny chef's coat I'd ordered from a children's dress-up shop.

Because even though Domovyks weren't exactly health code compliant, I had standards.

"Alright, Totally Teal, let's make some magic," I muttered, grabbing the brush and getting to work on the patched section of wall.

Elmo's Hardware had the good stuff, even if Elmo himself was an opinionated old Warlock who smelled vaguely of pickled herring.

I was almost done—just a little trim touch-up where I'd dripped—when I called, "Petyr, what time is it?"

"It is 7:22—"

"What?! I only have eight minutes to get across town!"

I shoved the paintbrush into his little hands.

"You finish this. And I know I said it's against the rules, but you're already holding the brush."

I tried to reason aloud for any Goddesses who might be listening.

"I will clean and lock up," he said with an uncharacteristically smug grin.

Honestly, he looked thrilled at the prospect, like I'd just promoted him to Domovyk-in-Charge.

I knew from my reading that Domovyks had once been worshipped as minor gods of the home, so maybe this was scratching some ancient itch for him.

Either way, I was grateful.

"Thanks, Petyr. You're the best," I said, bolting for the door.

"Oh damn. I'm late. I'm late. Oh damn. Oh damn," I muttered, tearing off my apron as I went.

Reminding myself of a certain white rabbit, I tore out of the bakery like my hair was on fire and my skirt was catching.

Only I didn't get far.

Because the universe clearly hates me.

All four tires on my car were flat.

Not low.

Not oh, maybe I should get those checked soft.

Flat.

"NO!"

I stomped my foot so hard the crack in the asphalt probably deepened.

First arson, now vandalism.

What next?

Would someone shave off my eyebrows in my sleep?

Leave a dead fish in my bread proofer?

Forget I even thought that.

Really. Please, forget it.

No sense in giving fate ideas.

I scanned the street, trying to figure out my options. I could run.

Except my legs are short, my boobs are big, and the combo turns into a cardio death trap real quick.

Plus, my chef's pants are not exactly made for speed.

I was two seconds away from despair when I heard it—*the deep, rumbling growl of an engine.*

A motorcycle.

Dang it.

I knew exactly who it was before I even turned around.

And I did not have time for this man.

Not tonight.

Not when the Trifecta was waiting on me in the clearing.

Not when I was still trying to figure out how to stop my heart from doing the cha-cha every time he came within six feet of me.

But there he was, all broad shoulders and sin incarnate, astride a gunmetal-gray motorcycle that looked like it had been built for seduction.

He wore dark jeans and scuffed leather boots, and his blond hair was tousled by the wind like he'd just ridden out of my dirtiest daydream.

I wanted to kick him in the shin for existing like that in public.

Then kiss him until we both forgot our own names.

Curse you, Witchy hormones.

"Hop on, Sugar. I'll get you to the clearing," he said, voice low and husky, like my name might be hidden in there somewhere if I just listened close enough.

It should've annoyed me—*being ordered around.*

It should've had me crossing my arms and telling him I could handle it myself, thank you very much.

Instead, well. It did *other* things to me.

Naughty things.

And when he leaned down and whispered, "Good girl," after I swung a leg over the bike and settled behind him?

I nearly melted into a puddle of Bella-flavored frosting right there in the seat.

"Fine," I muttered because dignity was important. "You can give me a ride. But it doesn't mean anything. Just get me there."

I even made a point of keeping my hands on the backrest like some kind of stubborn, apron-wearing rebel.

"Wrap your arms around my waist, Bella, and I'll get you there," he replied, like my snark didn't even graze him.

Ugh. The nerve.

He pressed on the gas—*the snake*—jerking me around a little. So yeah, I did it—I placed my hands on his waist. Lightly, barely touching him.

But even the barest brush of my fingers sent tingles racing up my arms.

My magic lit up like someone had plugged me into a socket.

It buzzed and hummed, practically purring at the contact.

See, my magic whispered. *We like him. We should keep him.*

Shut. Up.

I was not falling into whatever-this-was with a sexy-as-sin Snake man who looked like he'd been born for slow dancing in the dark and fast kisses in the kitchen.

"Tighter, Sugar. Wouldn't want you falling," he told me again, that growl-hiss rolling over me like a caress.

The second time he gunned it, I actually did grip him—*clawing him through his shirt*—pink and white sparks flared across my fingertips.

The tingles weren't just magic anymore. They were *him*. A heat that radiated from his body straight into mine.

And the worst part?

My attraction wasn't purely physical. I'd heard people talking about him—*how polite he was, how he went out of his way to help, how kids and grannies alike adored him.*

Which, of course, made it harder to convince myself he was bad news.

"Relationships are for the birds, Bella."

Granny's voice rang in my head, the same voice

that had carried me through more heartbreaks than I could count.

She'd also once said smart Witches didn't need men for anything but ingredients, which had been a deeply disturbing thing to hear as a child.

Especially a child who loved to cook.

But right now? Riding behind Conrad Boman, the wind whipping through my hair despite the helmet he'd buckled under my chin, I wasn't so sure Granny was right about this one.

The man was like gravity, pulling me to him with something magnetic I couldn't deny for much longer.

I mean, I was only human. *Well—Witch human.*

Sooner than I wanted him to, Conrad rolled that awesome motorcycle of his to a stop.

"Here you go. Safe and sound."

The words rumbled out of his chest and straight into mine. His body vibrated against mine, and for a second, I forgot we weren't still moving.

I was clinging to him like static, and he didn't seem in any hurry to pry me off.

Embarrassing.

We'd stopped at the edge of the trees guarding the clearing where my cousins were already waiting. I could hear Donny and Evie's voices from here—*low and wicked in that way only best friends can be.*

Judging from the way Conrad's mouth twitched, I had no doubt they were discussing exactly what they thought of me arriving on the back of his bike.

Saucy wenches. I grinned anyway.

The three of us were a package deal and we had the same ideals and agreed on things most of the time.

"Thank you," I said, finally forcing myself to let go.

Goddess, he was nice to touch.

All hard curves and heat and those long, dangerous fingers that could probably undo my self-control as easily as they could unlace my corset—*if I owned one.*

"Bella, I think we should talk—"

"No. No talking, Conrad. I just can't right now."

I tugged on my chef's pants to straighten them and—*of course*—got caught on something.

Ugh.

Because humiliation was my brand.

"Okay. Let me help you," he murmured, voice low enough to make my spine tingle.

Before I could protest—*or, you know, flee*—he swung one long leg over the motorcycle like some kind of leather-clad ballet dancer and crouched down in front of me.

My pant leg had gotten snagged on something near the foot peg, and apparently, this was his cue to play knight in shining denim.

"Thanks," I managed, trying to sound brisk and unbothered, even as I stood there frozen like I'd been hit with a body-bind spell.

Because here's the thing—*when Conrad Boman was this close, all my good sense packed up and went on vacation without me.*

My panties soaked. My chest heaved. And my entire being went on high alert.

"I know you have rules for a reason, Bella," he said, his head bent, deft fingers working at the fabric. "And I'm here if you ever want to discuss them. But just so you know—"

Oh no.

The *just so you know* tone was dangerous.

That was the tone of men who thought they were about to change your mind about something.

The tone of trouble.

And he was definitely trouble.

The sexy, square-jawed, snake-eyed kind of trouble my hormones insisted on throwing confetti over.

The fabric finally came free, and in one smooth, predator-like motion, Conrad stood. Blond waves fell into his face in that perfect, rockstar-messy way no man should be allowed to pull off outside of a shampoo commercial.

And yes.

Damn it.

He was hot.

Super hot.

The kind of hot you wanted to lick just to see if it burned.

Then, because the universe wanted me to suffer, the same hand that had freed my pant leg didn't immediately retreat. Oh, no.

It smoothed over my calf—slowly.

Then my knee.

Then higher.

By the time it grazed my hip, my body was staging a full-scale rebellion against my brain.

I had a thousand arguments for why this was a bad idea, but they were drowned out by one very loud, very inappropriate thought: *don't stop.*

And it was that thought—traitorous and wanton—that made me narrow my eyes at his ridiculously green gaze.

Because here was the truth, the one I hated

saying even in my own head: I didn't believe a man who looked like Conrad—*who could've been cast as a demigod in a blockbuster movie*—could ever be serious about someone like me.

Yes, I was cute.

Yes, I could bake circles around Martha Stewart in a throwdown.

But I wasn't built like the women who usually hung off the arms of men like him.

And Shifters, well, they were another species altogether when it came to physical perfection. Literally.

So why would I even try?

Sex was fun when it was good, and yes, he was *good*. But I wasn't looking to collect another broken heart just to add to the pile.

I opened my mouth, ready to tell him exactly that—ready to end this before it got dangerous—and without so much as a *by your leave*, the man *cupped the back of my neck*.

It was the hottest of all hot boy touches. The one book boyfriends the world over made if the author listened to the throngs of readers the world over when they wanted possessive sexy hot heroes to drool over.

But this wasn't a story.

This was one hundred percent real.

And I was so damn screwed.

Warm, strong fingers anchored me in place as he leaned in, closing the distance with that slow, inevitable gravity that made every nerve in my body light up.

Then his mouth was on mine.

It wasn't polite.

It wasn't brief.

It was a kiss that felt like he'd been planning it for a long time and didn't intend to waste a single second of it.

Rough, consuming, and so deep my magic sparked behind my eyelids, sending glittery pulses through my veins.

My toes curled so hard they might never uncurl.

My knees? Completely untrustworthy.

By the time he pulled back, I was breathless, disoriented, and possibly in another dimension.

"Sometimes all it takes is a leap of faith, Maribella," he murmured, and then—*just like that*—he was gone.

No lingering glance.

No cocky grin.

Just the roar of his motorcycle as he rode away,

leaving me standing there like some lovesick extra in the music video of my own life.

Granny always said relationships were for the birds.

But as the growl of his engine faded—*or maybe that was just the thundering of my heart*—I had to wonder.

Maybe relationships were for the Snakes.

And maybe, just maybe if I was very, very lucky, they were for Witches, too.

CHAPTER THIRTEEN-BELLA

"SO, is it like dirty-water hot dog dong—long and slim—or like broccoli rabe sausage dong—thick and fat? Come on, what are we talking about here?" Donny asked Evie in a voice that carried across the clearing like she was auditioning for Witch Gossip Hour.

I came crashing into the moonlit space, lungs burning, hair sticking to my cheeks, huffing, and puffing like a third-rate forest nymph who'd failed cardio class.

"Definitely more like the sausage," Evie replied without missing a beat, "but still long. Thick though, too. Like maybe three of them tied together! OMG, Donny, for fuck's sake. The man's a Shifter—oooh!

You finally made it!" Evie screeched, spinning toward me like I was the guest of honor at a scandal.

"Look who showed up! Snake got your tongue, Miss Maribella?" Donny sing-songed, her grin wicked enough to make a demon blush.

"Shut up," I muttered, kicking off my shoes before my feet staged a mutiny.

"She's just jealous 'cause we were talking dongs, and she hasn't seen one in a while, right, Bella?" Donny said, smirking like she'd been waiting all week for this moment.

"FYI, Ryan is packing, ladies! And in a Bear-sized way. So, Bella, how long's it been since you've seen a good ding-dong? We talking months or years?"

"Heifers," I grunted, peeling my socks off with the kind of grim determination reserved for marathon runners and women trying to get out of Spanx.

"Not that long. And if you two are done talking about your men and their puny wangs, can we get down to business? The moon is rising, and we are one month from the summer solstice."

"They do not have puny wangs!" Evie snarled—*literally snarled*—at me, her upper lip curling like a Wolf about to pounce.

I blinked.

Well.

That was *a lot.*

"You okay there, Cujo?" I asked, because apparently my mouth had no self-preservation instinct tonight.

Her eyes widened like she'd just realized she'd barked at me—almost literally—and she immediately softened.

"Um, sorry about the growling," she muttered, her hand drifting to her stomach like she was checking herself for signs of lycanthropy.

I gave her a curious look but didn't press. I was too busy shucking my clothes with the speed of a chubby girl who knew the night air wasn't going to get any warmer.

And yeah, my cheeks were on fire.

Was it because of the frustratingly short yet toe-curling kiss I'd gotten from Conrad like seconds ago?

Was it embarrassment at having my best friends dissect my non-existent sex life in high-definition detail?

Or was it just the fact I'd sprinted across town on a motorcycle with a hot Snake Man like a Witch with her broom on fire?

Probably all three.

"Ease up, Evie. We've got work to do," Donny said, her tone carrying that bossy-big-sister energy she liked to whip out whenever she thought one of us was about to spiral.

That was the thing about us—no matter how much we teased each other, we had each other's backs.

I might want to occasionally strangle them both with a festive ribbon, but I wouldn't trade either of them for the world.

"Sorry, really, guys. I don't know what's wrong with me," Evie said softly, her eyes shadowed.

"That's okay," I said with a shrug and a grin to make sure she knew I meant it. "I didn't mean to be almost late."

That seemed to reset the mood.

We all shifted into work mode, the air thickening with the warm hum of our combined magic.

This wasn't just a monthly ritual—*it was our duty. Our privilege.*

Evie, our de facto leader, was a veritable Seer Witch.

She could catch glimpses of the future, though personally, I wasn't convinced it was as much of a gift as she claimed.

If I knew a pie was going to burn before it did, sure, that would be useful—but seeing every tragedy on the horizon?

Hard pass.

Still, maybe that's why she was mayor, and I was the town's cookie dealer.

Whatever. I wouldn't trade with her.

Donny's magic was a little more like mine—practical, rooted in her work.

As the best hair stylist in Castor's Corner (and possibly the tri-state area), she could see straight into a person's soul and give them the cut they didn't even know they needed.

The kind of haircut that could make you forget you ever dated your loser ex, start a new career, and maybe even run for office.

Me? I fed people.

Nourished them—*literally, spiritually, and magically.*

Cookies, cakes, croissants, cinnamon rolls—you name it, I baked it. Each treat was infused with a little magic and a whole lot of feeling, gifting whoever ate it with comfort, joy, or the tiniest spark of hope.

And tonight, the three of us would pour our magic into the wards that kept Castor's Corner hidden from mortal eyes.

Which, yes, we did completely bare-assed around a roaring pink bonfire.

And yes, it did look like a magical conga line sometimes.

Afterward, there'd be a lemon bar tasting at my place—my latest zero-carb experiment.

I thought I'd nailed it this time, but I wasn't ready to brag until Evie and Donny tried them.

Last time I got creative with *healthy* recipes, my cinnamon hot cocoa bombs turned into literal explosives the moment they hit hot milk.

We were still finding chocolate shrapnel in Donny's sitting room months later.

My bad.

Anyway, I was knee-deep in one of my many obsessions—*holistic baking*.

Not the fake diet crap that made everything taste like cardboard dipped in regret, but the real deal.

Natural sugar substitutions, whole grains, nut flours, gluten-free blends I'd sworn I'd never touch in my life—parts of my kitchen looked like a hippie's pantry and smelled like heaven.

It was exciting. Scary. Like dating again after a bad breakup, only this time the relationship was with einkorn flour and monk fruit sweetener instead of some guy who thought turkey bacon counted as romance.

I'd swapped out the white flour completely in my carrot cake last week.

Not one single complaint.

Not even from Mrs. Gennaro, who could detect a missing teaspoon of cinnamon from ten paces and had the resting face of a food critic.

That was basically a Michelin star in my world.

"Light her up, Donny," I said, moving to my exact spot in our ritual triangle.

And no, assuming the position wasn't dirty—so once again, please, get your mind out of the gutter.

This was work. Sacred work.

We each stood with feet spread shoulder-width apart, arms open wide, palms up, chins tilted toward the star-smeared sky.

The fire pit in the center of the clearing was just waiting for ignition, surrounded by moonlit pines and the faint shimmer of the town's protective wards.

We'd stripped down to nothing.

No clothes. No jewelry. No hair ties.

Even my lucky cupcake-print ankle socks had been sacrificed to the ritual.

Naked magic was potent magic—something about energy flow and unimpeded channels.

Plus, the Goddess had a sense of humor about cellulite.

Or so I prayed.

The moment Donny's fingers snapped and the fire roared to life in a ribbon of shimmering pink flame, the air grew heavy with heat and power.

It licked over my skin, raising goosebumps, the scent of woodsmoke and ozone wrapping around us like an embrace.

"I just want to reiterate Jaxson has a big dong," Evie muttered, eyes closed like she was talking to the Goddess herself.

I cracked one eye open. "Shhh!" I hissed. "Some of us are trying to focus."

Because if I lost concentration and accidentally pictured our Wolf Shifter Sheriff's alleged *endowment* while I was channeling magic, the wards might just start humming Barry White.

"Ryan does too," Donny whispered, her voice all faux-innocence, like she didn't know exactly what she was doing to my concentration.

"*Ohmyfuckinggawd,*" I growled, literally growled, as pink sparks fizzed and popped off my fingertips.

My magic wasn't subtle—*it was basically a glitter cannon with a temper.*

"Fine. Yes. Your boyfriends have massive wieners, okay?"

"Eww. Don't say wiener," Evie said, her nose wrinkling like I'd just dumped a can of sardines in her smoothie.

I dropped my arms, turning toward them with my tatas swaying in the evening breeze like I was about to stage a naked protest.

"By the Goddess, okay! Fine. No to the word wieners. How about penises when referring to your mates' *nethers*?"

"She said penises," Donny snorted, shoulders shaking, eyes still closed like she was somehow still meditating through her laughter.

"Fine! No to penises," I snapped, though my lips were twitching. "Then how about this: your dudes have dongs—not regular dongs—but *MEGLADONGS*. There. Happy now? Can we get on with this, you heifers?"

That was when Evie just stared at me.

Wide-eyed.

Mouth hanging open like she'd just witnessed a Coven elder say *glass dildo* at the Harvest Feast.

Donny didn't even try to hide her laughter this time—she let it out in one loud, Witch-cackle snort.

Which was exactly when a jagged streak of pink lightning ripped across the sky.

The hair on my arms stood up.

The fire crackled like it had been insulted.

Uh-oh.

I knew that sound.

That feeling.

That warning.

Somewhere, the Goddess was side-eyeing me.

And if I wasn't careful, my next batch of croissants was going to spontaneously combust just to teach me a lesson.

That pink lightning bolt still sizzled in my memory when I muttered a quick apology to the Goddess and cleared my throat.

Any more distractions and we'd be rolling around the clearing in a fit of naked giggles until sunrise.

That wasn't exactly the kind of magic we were here to make.

"Okay, back to business," I said, shaking my head and clapping my hands together before the two of them could launch another sausage-based debate.

Resuming my stance, I started the chant in fluent Ork—thank you, *Drusilla Bartholomew Frankenstein*

Yaganova's Magical Language Academy Version 3.7, and yes, that's a real thing.

Troll-Tongue might sound like a curse you'd yell after stubbing your toe, but in our line of work? It got results.

Evie joined in quickly, her voice dropping into the low, thrumming cadence we needed, and Donny fell right in step.

Thank the Goddess—because my mind had been drifting to the exact wrong place. Again.

Ever since Conrad rolled into town with Jaxson and Ryan, I'd been distracted.

And not just in the casual "oh, he's hot" kind of way.

No, the man had my brain doing gymnastics and my body signing up for events it didn't even train for.

I could handle sex.

I was good at keeping it fun, uncomplicated. But Conrad wanted more.

Be with me, Bella. Accept my claim.

The first time he'd said that, I'd laughed.

The tenth time, I'd practically sprinted out the back door of my bakery.

The man had to be confused. Sure, we had chemistry—*dangerously good chemistry*—but fate?

Mating? Forever?

That wasn't real for everyone.

And it wasn't part of *my* story.

At least, that's what I told myself.

"Bella. Focus."

Evie's sharp tone yanked me back, and I shut the door on every image of broad shoulders and sinfully full lips.

I threw myself into the chant and the movement, letting the rhythm push everything else out of my head.

The three of us fell into that perfect, ancient groove.

Our magic braided together—Evie's gold, Donny's aqua, my pink—curling upward like a living ribbon around the roaring bonfire.

Sparks shimmered in the air, and the scent of charmed cedar and lilac drifted through the clearing.

By the time the power crested, I was breathless and grinning, my magic humming like I'd just downed a double espresso.

"Okay, Witches, I think we did it! Good for another month!" Evie's voice was bright, triumphant.

Donny whooped.

I dropped into the grass, too wrung out to care that my butt was in the dirt.

The air was cool on my bare skin, and my heartbeat still felt synced to the thrum of the wards.

Evie, always the practical one, tossed me one of her silk robes. "Come on, robe up before you get chilled."

I slid into it, sighing at the feel of the smooth fabric against my overheated skin.

Wildflowers in deep jewel tones swirled over the dark green silk—it was so Evie.

Then I heard it—the low rumble of engines heading our way.

And just like that, the temperature in the clearing seemed to climb ten degrees.

Evie's face lit up the second Jaxson's cruiser pulled in.

She didn't even wait for him to get the door open before she was moving toward him, and his answering whistle—*yeah, an actual Wolf whistle*—made her giggle like a teenager.

Right behind him, Ryan rolled up on his bike, all broad shoulders and gruff heat.

"There's my honey," he rumbled before lifting Donny clean off her feet.

She laughed in that high, unguarded way I hadn't heard in years.

I smiled without meaning to, even as something in my chest pulled tight.

They had their people. Their mates.

And me? I had my robe, my lemon bars, and an empty kitchen waiting at home.

I bent to scoop up my clothes, hugging them to my chest.

No way was I asking for a ride wedged between one of my besties and her panting, overprotective Shifter.

I'd walk before I did that.

And if that meant a mile of pink bits in the breeze, well, at least it wasn't snowing.

Evie glanced over her shoulder. "You did good tonight, Bella."

"We all did," Donny added.

"Thanks," I said, managing a smile.

But as they turned back to their men, I caught Evie's hand drifting to her belly again.

A thought hit me hard—*if they started families, if they had kids, everything would change.*

I'd still be here, but I'd be on the outside looking in.

I turned down the path toward home, the sound of laughter and kisses following me.

You made your choice, I reminded myself.

Single was safe.

Single was simple.

But for the first time in a long while, I wasn't sure if *safe* was enough.

Everything good starts with a leap of faith.

CHAPTER FOURTEEN-CONRAD

THE WOODS WERE black velvet and silver moonlight, every branch and shadow a familiar part of my body.

I moved through them without a sound, without a single leaf or twig betraying my presence.

In this skin, my scales drank the night.

The cold air slid along my length as I wound silently between the trees, the rhythm of my muscles a steady, patient pulse.

Her scent was everywhere—sugar and sweet vanilla blended with hints of citrus, and that soft, unmistakable thread of magic that made my instincts sharpen and soften all at once.

I could hear her before I saw her, though not in the usual way.

She didn't know it, but her magic sang, a quiet hum through the ground and air.

Each note was a breadcrumb leading me closer.

And there she was.

Bella.

Standing just outside the clearing now, robe loose around her, hair mussed from the wind, skin still glowing from the ritual fire.

She was laughing with her friends, but it wasn't the same laugh she gave when no one else was watching.

That laugh—*her real laugh*—was for the rare moments when she let herself be unguarded.

I wanted that.

I wanted all of her.

I curled tighter into the shadows, unseen.

Her hearing might be sharp, but I was sharper.

Scales didn't rustle.

My Python's body barely displaced the air.

She could have been surrounded by a dozen creatures, and I still would've been the only one to slip past her notice.

I stayed just inside the tree line, where the flicker of the moon caught on my pattern.

Watching her hips sway when she shifted her weight.

Watching her tug her robe a little tighter, like she could guard herself against the night—and me.

She thought she could keep me at a distance, keep me locked out of whatever walls she'd built.

But I'd been waiting my whole life for her, and I had the kind of patience only a predator knew.

I could wait another night.

Another week.

But not forever.

I let my tongue taste the air—warm skin, baked sugar, and a trace of lemon from whatever she'd been working on before the ritual.

Goddess, she smelled good enough to swallow whole.

Soon.

I could picture it already. Standing close enough to feel her breath hitch, close enough to tuck that stray hair behind her ear, close enough to cup her jaw and make her look at me—*really look at me*—and see that I wasn't letting go.

Please, Bella. Let me in.

My coils shifted over the moss, silent as breath, and I followed her retreat down the road from the clearing, never more than a few paces back.

Guarding.

Worshipping.

Counting down the minutes until I could do it up close, my hands on her instead of just my eyes.

For now, I'd take this—shadow and distance and the privilege of watching her move through the world like she didn't have a man in the dark who would burn it all down for her.

Even though she did.

See, I was that man. Her man. The only one created specifically for the purpose of loving her.

And one day soon, she was going to know it.

Yesssss. Mine.

CHAPTER FIFTEEN-BELLA

THE WALK HOME WAS LONG, and my skin was still tingling—not the fun, post-bonfire glow kind of tingle, but the itchy, restless kind that made me feel like I'd just swallowed an entire espresso shot of magic.

Every nerve felt raw and alive.

I told myself it was from the ritual.

I told myself it wasn't from him.

I was a damned liar.

The pine barrens stretched out around me, moonlight slicing through the trees in silver ribbons.

The air was cool enough to raise goosebumps on my bare arms, but I didn't slow down.

Couldn't stay stuck out here all night.

My soul felt heavy.

My body ached in that bone-deep way that came from holding too much inside.

I knew exactly what was wrong with me.

I missed Conrad, I just didn't want to admit it.

"You always walk home alone, Sugar?"

The voice slid in from my right—*low, husky, threaded with something that made my stomach drop to my knees.*

I yelped and almost tripped over a knotted tree root.

My robe fluttered open a dangerous inch before I caught myself, heat flooding my cheeks.

Where the hell had he come from?

One second, I was alone with my thoughts. The next, Conrad was there—close enough that the heat from his body brushed against my skin in waves.

My heart tried to beat its way out of my chest.

I knew he and his friends were staying in the little cottage behind my bakery and that I'd pass it on my way home. That was, the guys had *all* lived there before Ryan moved in with Donny and Jaxson with Evie.

Now it was just him, but he might as well have been a ghost.

Bakery hours didn't leave much room for casual drop-ins, and Conrad didn't strike me as a man who did anything casually.

I hadn't seen him for days, now twice today, and I didn't know what to think.

The rental was only a few rows down from my own two-story Colonial, which was why I decided to come home from the other direction.

So I didn't have to pass him.

Fat lot of good that did.

Poof! There he was again, materializing out of the dark like he'd been part of the forest all along.

I didn't see his motorcycle. No truck. Not Deputy's car, either. Which was unnerving because I knew he drove all three.

I baked cookies for the man who handled all of Castor's Corners mechanical needs.

Anyway, how had Conrad gotten here without his vehicles? And why?

"Yep. Walking it is," I said, aiming for casual but sounding slightly breathless. "I didn't drive myself tonight."

He knew that, of course.

But he just made a low sound in his throat, one of those noncommittal man-noises that somehow carried more weight than an entire sentence.

He kept pace with me for a few more steps before his hand—*warm, strong*—closed around my elbow.

"Can I see you to your door, Bella?"

The way he said my name? Like it was a promise and a curse all at once. Well, it did things to me.

I pretended to think it over, though the truth was obvious.

Who wouldn't want a six-foot-plus wall of Shifter muscle walking them through town in the middle of the night?

Especially when said Witch was wearing nothing but a robe and a stubborn streak.

"Fine," I said, trying to sound like I was doing him a favor. "But it's just a walk, Conrad. Don't read anything into it."

His smirk was slow and dangerous, curling at one corner of his mouth.

"Anything you say, Sugar. But just so you know," he leaned in close enough that his breath brushed my ear. "I'm up for anything with you, anytime. Day or night."

Panty. Melting. Statement.

Ugh.

The walk to my front door was far too short for my liking—because of course, now that I'd decided to let him walk me, I wasn't ready for him to leave.

I turned to face him and nearly swallowed my own tongue.

He was barefoot, wearing only a pair of black sweats, his skin still glistening faintly from a shift.

The moonlight slid over his chest, lighting up the ridges and valleys of muscle in a way that should've been illegal.

His hair—*those ridiculous blond waves*—looked like he'd run his hands through them right before walking out to find me.

I inhaled, and warm breezes mixed with the sharp green scent of the grass and that deep, heady musk that was all Conrad.

"Um, thanks for this," I murmured, wishing I had any excuse to keep him standing there.

Unless.

"Hey, are you hungry?"

The corner of his mouth tipped up again, but his eyes—*Goddess, his eyes*—were all heat and singular focus.

"Hungry? Me? Always, Sugar."

The words were harmless enough.

The way he said them was absolutely, one hundred percent *not*.

"Good. I had Petyr bring home some lemon bars from the bakery earlier today." I tucked a piece of hair behind my ear, trying not to fidget. "I'm, uh, trying out a new recipe."

"Oh?" His voice dipped even lower, like he already knew he had me where he wanted me. "Lemon's my favorite."

"Is it?" I tilted my head, pretending it was news to me.

But I'd known.

Of course I'd known.

I paid attention when it came to him, no matter how hard I tried not to.

"So, would you like to come in and try a couple? Let me know if they're up to par?"

There.

The invitation was out there, hanging in the night air between us. The rest was up to him.

If he said no, I'd survive. Probably.

If he said yes, well, my robe wasn't the only thing about to come undone.

"Oh, I don't know. You said this was just a walk, Maribella. I wouldn't want you to think I was being pushy or anything."

His tone was all mock innocence, but those raised brows and that smirk told another story entirely.

"Fine," I growled, throwing my door open with

more force than necessary.

My robe swished around my thighs, and I stomped—*yes, stomped*—up the walkway.

Not gracefully.

Not with any kind of sultry sway.

Just solid, irritated footfalls that said if you don't want my goodies, then you don't get my goodies.

I didn't make it halfway to the porch before he was suddenly there.

"I didn't say no, Bella," Conrad murmured, right in front of me.

Goddess, help me, he moved like water—*smooth, inevitable, and impossible to stop.*

I'd been around Shifters before, but there was something about the way he covered ground that felt more like sorcery than speed.

One second, he was yards away, the next he was filling my vision, his firm, warm hand closing around my elbow.

My magic reacted before I could stop it—*pink sparks skittering under my skin, heat curling low in my belly.*

"Up to you," I mumbled, unwilling to meet his gaze because I knew if I did, I'd drown in those emerald eyes.

I slipped free of his touch and led the way up the

cobblestone path. My deep burgundy door stood out against the beige siding like a bold lipstick choice on bare skin.

Inside, the space reflected my moods.

A buttery yellow kitchen with a monster eight-burner stove and four ovens.

Cozy natural wood cabinets with frosted glass doors.

A living room designed with calming blues and grays.

And finally, my bedroom, which was done in all soft mauves and cream.

Comfortable. Safe. Mine.

A flick of my fingers and a shimmer of pink-white magic unlocked the door, my wards whispering their approval.

The Draco Fortis security system—*a blend of cutting-edge technology and old-world spellcraft designed by a Dragon Shifter who lived not too far from Castor's Corner in Maccon City*—hummed quietly in the background.

The place smelled faintly of lemon sugar and home.

"Smells great in here, Sugar," Conrad said, stepping in close enough to brush a kiss over my cheek.

It wasn't a hungry kiss—*not yet*—but my skin still flared hot at the contact.

"Follow me," I managed, keeping my voice

neutral, even as my heart was trying to beat a hole in my ribs.

In the kitchen, I busied myself plating a couple of lemon bars, pretending I couldn't feel his eyes on me. "Tea?"

"That would be great, Maribella," he said, voice husky enough to slide right under my robe.

The kettle went on.

The scent of fresh-cut lemon and warm sugar filled the space between us.

He smelled of pine needles, damp earth, and something sharper—clean, wild air that made me think of the pine barrens where I'd just been.

Had he been there, watching?

It was a Shifter thing—*staying close to their mates.*

Except Conrad wasn't my mate.

I had to keep telling myself that.

He bit into the lemon bar, and the deep, masculine sound he made in his throat nearly buckled my knees.

"These are fantastic," he said around the second bite. "Did I already tell you lemon's my favorite? Good Goddess, woman, I could eat the whole tray."

"I know. I mean about lemon being your favorite," I admitted before I could stop myself.

His grin was slow and wicked, like he knew exactly how much attention I paid to him.

And maybe he was right.

I watched as a smear of lemon filling clung to his pinky.

He caught me looking, and instead of grabbing a napkin like a normal person, he brought his hand to his mouth.

And licked.

The tip of his tongue swirled, slow and deliberate, before he drew it into his mouth and sucked the last trace away.

My mouth went dry.

Because I knew that tongue.

Knew what it could do.

Knew what it felt like when he shifted that part of him, forking that long, muscled appendage and tasting me with it.

Heat coiled low and tight between my legs, my robe suddenly feeling like the thinnest, most dangerous thing I owned.

My nipples peaked against the silk, my breathing quickening.

Conrad's gaze darkened, the green deepening to a molten emerald.

"You've got something on your lip, Sugar."

Before I could swipe at it, he was there—*closing the space, his thumb brushing my mouth.*

Not a quick wipe, but a slow, lingering drag that had my lips parting on instinct.

His hand was warm, rough in all the right ways, and my body leaned toward his without my permission.

"You want me to get the rest?" he asked softly.

I should have said no.

Should have laughed it off.

Instead, I whispered, "Yes."

And his mouth was on mine—soft at first, teasing, like he was testing how far I'd let him go.

Then deeper, hungrier, the taste of lemon and sugar mixing with the heady, male taste of him.

My hands found his bare chest, the heat of his skin scorching my palms.

When his tongue brushed mine—*just the faintest flicker of that forked edge*—I moaned into his mouth.

It had been weeks since we'd touched, and my body remembered every single detail.

Every thrust, every shiver, every pulse of magic that sparked between us.

The kettle whistled shrilly behind me, but neither of us moved.

Because tea could wait.

But Conrad?

Conrad wasn't the kind of man you made wait when he kissed you like this.

And the truth was, I didn't want to wait either.

CHAPTER SIXTEEN-CONRAD

SHE SMELLED like sugar and magic and something I'd never been able to get enough of. I could taste her in the air, feel the thrum of her power like static against my skin.

Every damn time I got close, my Python rose up inside me with one single thought.

Mine.

And she was.

Even if she didn't believe it yet.

I'd been patient—hell, for a Shifter like me, I'd been a saint.

But watching her move around her kitchen, robe clinging in all the right places, her magic still sparking faintly over her skin from the ritual earlier, *yeah*, I was about one deep breath away from forgetting every promise I'd made myself about giving her time.

"What's rattling around that pretty head of yours, Sugar? You're positively permeating pheromones," I murmured, leaning in close enough to take a long, slow inhale.

Goddess, she smelled like warm lemon sugar and desire.

She tossed me a sidelong look, chin tilted.

"Wouldn't you like to know?"

"Damn straight, I would," I growled, stepping in behind her before she could sidestep me.

Her body went still—except for that tiny tremor I felt when I let my arousal press against her lower body.

She knew exactly what she was doing to me.

My mind flashed back to the last time I'd been buried inside her, the way she'd clutched at me like I was the only thing tethering her to the earth.

I'd never forget that.

Never wanted to.

I dipped my head, brushing my lips over the warm, soft skin just below her ear.

She moaned—*quiet, but enough to gut me*—and my control frayed another inch.

My tongue flicked out, tasting her, before I nipped at her lobe and spun her to face me.

"I want to know everything about you, sweet Witch," I told her, and meant it.

Not just her body—*though, yeah, I wanted that too, every damn day*—but the things she thought were too small or too silly to matter.

The things no one else got to see.

She didn't even hesitate.

"I'm a Virgo and eating is my love language."

I laughed, low and genuine.

"Ha ha! Good to know. We have the eating thing in common, but my choice of delights is likely different."

I let the suggestion roll off my tongue, slow and deliberate, watching the way her pupils blew wide.

Then I kissed her jaw, trailing little nips toward her mouth. She opened for me, but I didn't rush it—I teased.

Let her chase me.

And when she backed off, I followed, because there was no world where I could let her pull away.

"I want all of it, Maribella," I murmured between feather-light brushes of our lips. "Every last one of your secrets. Mine. But I can be patient. I'll wait for you to be ready."

Her eyes were glazed, her voice distracted.

"Ready for what?"

Oh, she knew.

Her magic was singing to mine, wrapping us both in a slow, burning coil.

My Python was pacing just under my skin, restless and hungry.

I cupped her face, tilting it up until those dark eyes were locked on mine.

"Ready for us."

And then I kissed her the way I'd been dying to—*hard, deep, like I could brand her soul with the taste of me.*

Her body melted into mine, soft and warm and wanting.

Sparks flared where our skin touched, and I knew she felt it too.

That connection.

That rightness.

I'd had lovers before. Special ones. Good ones.

But they were nothing compared to Bella.

She. Was. Everything.

This wasn't about getting off—*though, fuck, she could ruin me without even trying*—this was about claiming something I knew down to my bones was supposed to be mine.

"Bella," I groaned against her mouth, because I needed her to hear it, needed her to know.

"Wanna give you everything you want, sweet Witch. Don't you know how hard it is for me to stay away?"

Her answer was breathless, dangerous.

"Then don't."

The sound of her heartbeat thudding inside her soft, sweet body filled the space between us, and my control snapped.

"You're my mate, Maribella Strega," I said roughly. "I know you don't believe me, but it's true."

She tilted her head, mouth curving in that way that made me both crazy and weak.

"How do you know that?"

"A Shifter knows. My Python knew the second I saw you—"

"Wait, which Python? This one?" she teased, her hand slipping into my sweats and closing around me with a firm, slow stroke.

My eyes slammed shut.

"Fuck. Yes, that one. But also the other one."

"I see," she purred, dragging her tongue along my neck until I thought I might lose the ability to stand.

"Bella," I growled, grabbing her wrist before I lost it completely. "If you don't stop, I'm going to take you right here. I'm trying to be a gentleman and give you space, but I'm only human." I paused, correcting with a feral grin. "Partly."

"What if I don't want any more space between us tonight, Big Guy?"

And just like that.

I was wrecked.

Still, I had to ask.

Just had to push the envelope.

Even though her answer just might kill me.

"What are you saying, Bella? Will you let me claim you, Mate?"

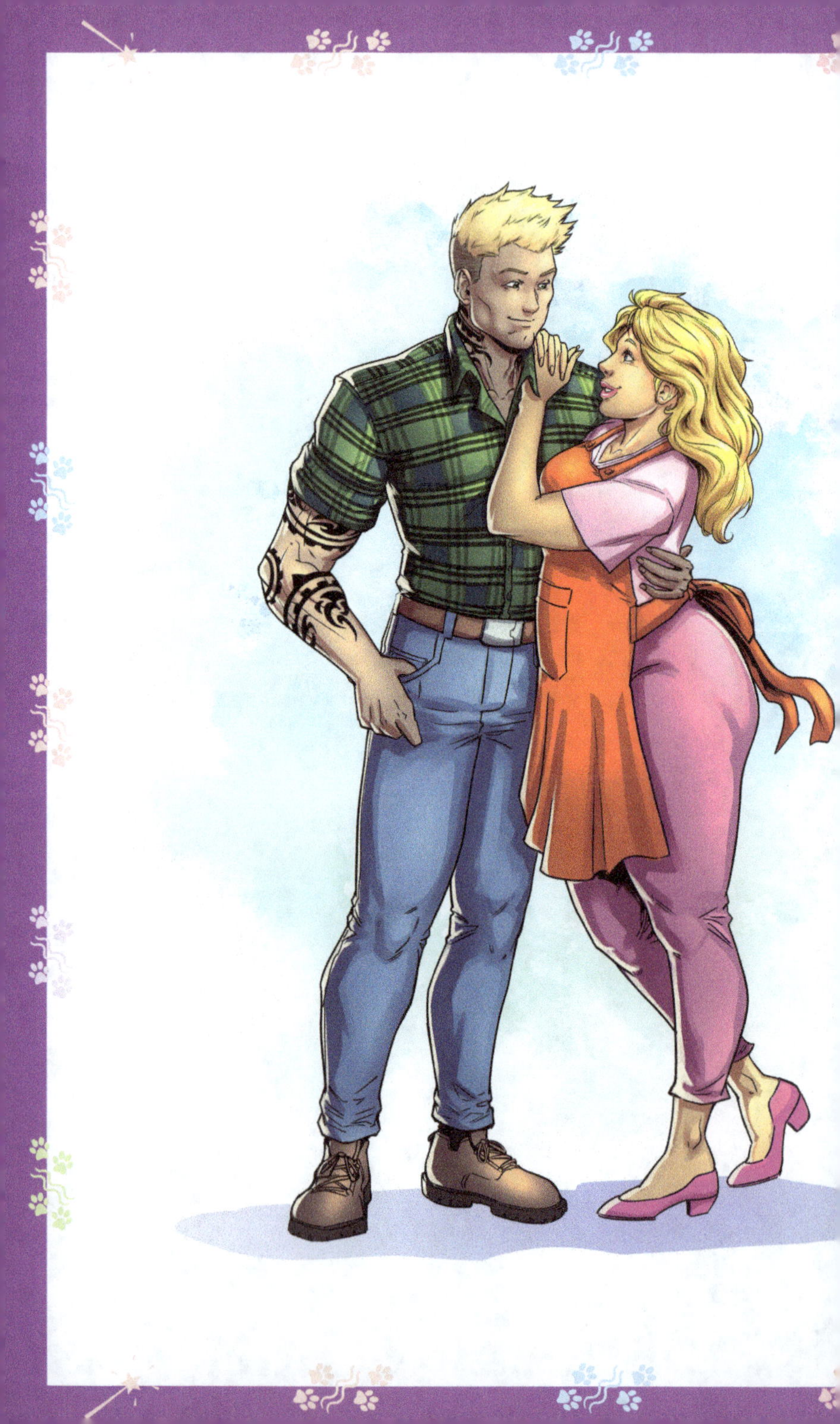

CHAPTER SEVENTEEN-BELLA

I FROZE FOR A SECOND, my palm still wrapped around the thick, pulsing length of him.

His words hung between us like a live wire, crackling with possibility and danger.

Mate.

That was the real kicker though.

That one word sent a shiver down my spine that had nothing to do with the cool air drifting through the kitchen window and everything to do with the way his body felt under my hand—*hot, alive, mine.*

Was he right? Was I really his mate?

My brain wanted to be skeptical, logical, cautious.

But my body? Oh, Goddess, my body was a traitor.

It was already singing in tune with him, every nerve lit up, every cell leaning toward him like a plant to the sun.

His kiss.

His touch.

The deep, aching joy that bloomed in my chest when I was with him. I didn't have that with anyone else. Ever.

My fingers flexed, squeezing his thick cock gently, reveling in the heat of him, the silky-smooth skin over the hard, heavy ridge beneath.

It felt right.

Like my hand was made to fit him.

Like I belonged there.

And that terrified me.

"I don't have an answer for that yet," I heard myself say, voice low and shaky. "But I want you. I need you. I just need time, okay?"

"Time?"

His mouth grazed mine between kisses, his breath warm and laced with that faint, wild scent that was all Conrad.

"Yes. Time. I just, I don't know if I'm ready to try this whole mate thing on."

"Bella," he groaned like I was hurting him. "That's not how it is—"

"Conrad, I just, look I want to be with you. What if, like maybe, we can just see each other a while?"

His brow lifted.

But he wasn't pushing me away, so that was good, right?

"So, you want to what? Date me?"

"Exactly. You know what I mean—*ohhh*," I moaned as his big hand slid mine away and swept me off my feet like I weighed nothing.

I gasped, legs automatically winding around his waist as he pressed his lips to my earlobe.

I'd forgotten how strong he was—forgotten the sheer thrill of being lifted and held like I was precious, like I was his.

Oh my, a Witch could get used to this.

"First," he said, voice low and gravelly, "if we're dating, it's exclusive. Agreed?"

He punctuated the question by sliding one hand under my robe, finding my nipple with unerring accuracy.

His fingers rolled the sensitive peak, sending a bolt of pleasure straight between my thighs.

My head thunked back, saved from the wall by Conrad's quick fingers, and I whimpered.

"Yes. Yes, agreed," I blurted, the words spilling

out before I could think, because thinking was impossible when my body was screaming for him to keep going.

"Second," he murmured, eyes glittering, "while we're dating, I have full rein to pursue your acceptance of my claim. I plan to seduce you, Bella, but only because you are already mine."

"You Snake," I accused, breathless. "You're going to use my weakness for you against me."

"Damn straight," he growled, catching my bottom lip in his teeth, then soothing it with a lazy sweep of his tongue.

My toes curled.

My knees might've gone weak if he wasn't already holding me up.

"I'm going to love on this luscious body of yours until you have no choice but to believe me when I tell you. You. Are. Mine."

Before I could form a comeback, his mouth claimed mine—*hard, hungry, no more teasing*—and his hands were everywhere, tugging my robe off my shoulders, baring me to the cool air and his heated gaze.

Then his sweats were pushed down, and the blunt head of his cock slid along my slick folds.

I bit back a cry.

"You're so fucking wet," he hissed against my mouth.

Of course I was.

He was hotter than the sun, and I'd been aching for this for weeks.

"No more sweet talk, Con. Fuck me already," I demanded, my voice a ragged mix of need and surrender.

"I can do that, Ssssugar," he hissed.

One sharp thrust and he was inside me, stretching me, filling me until I could hardly breathe.

My nails dug into his shoulders, clinging as wave after wave of pleasure rolled through me.

"That's my girl," he growled, moving with that sinuous, powerful rhythm that made my vision blur. "Give it all to me."

It didn't take long—*my orgasm hit like a lightning strike, my body clenching around him in desperate, pulsing waves.*

My legs went shaky, but Conrad wasn't done.

He set me down just long enough to spin me toward the wall, planting my palms flat on the cool surface.

His hands gripped my hips, tugging me back against him until I was perfectly positioned.

Then he drove into me again.

The sound he made—*a deep, animalistic hiss-slash-growl*—rolled through me like thunder.

He leaned forward, caging me in as he whispered things in my ear that would make a Demon blush, each word punctuated by a sharp thrust.

When he fisted my ponytail and turned my head for a kiss mid-stroke, I nearly came again on the spot.

And then I did. Hard.

My whole body trembled as I clenched around him, and moments later, he followed with a guttural groan, spilling deep inside me.

I sagged against the wall, panting, wondering how the hell I was supposed to get upstairs on legs made of jelly.

Conrad, apparently, had no doubts.

He wiped me clean with a warm, wet paper towel —*sweet, surprisingly tender*—and when I started to fumble for words, he cut me off with a wicked smirk.

"That was—" I began.

"Only the first round, Sugar. I hope you had a good dinner," he said, scooping me up princess-style before kissing me until my head spun all over again.

I let out a breathless laugh.

"Not really."

"Guess I'll have to feed you between rounds," he murmured, carrying me toward the stairs like I weighed nothing.

He kissed me the second his feet hit the first stair. And he didn't stop. Not until we made it to the bedroom.

By the time he finally lifted his head, I was limp, lusty, and grinning like a fool.

At some point between the sex and the scrambled eggs he made me afterward, it hit me—*Conrad Boman wasn't just in my bed.*

He was my boyfriend.

Or maybe my mate.

And for the first time, I wasn't sure which idea scared me more.

No. Not my mate.

Not yet.

And that was my choice.

I could almost feel the word hovering in the air between us—*mate*—a promise and a prison all in one, depending on how you looked at it.

Conrad believed it with every fiber of his being, but I wasn't ready to step over that line, not when my heart had only just started to believe it might be safe in someone's hands again.

Still he was special.

Not just in the *sweet-talks-you-out-of-your-panties* kind of way—*though, trust me, he excelled at that*—but in the way he looked at me like I was worth the effort.

Like my curves, my sass, my magic, my me were not just tolerable but treasured.

Even if he only stayed a little while, I knew I would never regret what we'd just shared.

The way his hands had roamed over my body like he was mapping constellations.

The way his voice had gone rough and low when he whispered my name like a prayer.

Fear tried to sneak in—*sharp and cold, whispering that things this good don't last, that people leave, that bonds break*—but I shoved it back down where it belonged.

I refused to let it ruin this.

I didn't know how long this thing between us would last, and maybe that was the point.

Maybe the beauty of it was in not knowing.

So I made a silent vow right then, as he lay beside me, still warm and breathing steady, one arm draped possessively across my waist.

I would enjoy my time with Conrad Boman.

Every heated look.

Every stolen kiss.

Every lazy morning tangled in sheets and limbs.

Every. Last. Second.

Because if the day came when he walked away, I wanted my memories so full they'd leave no room for regret.

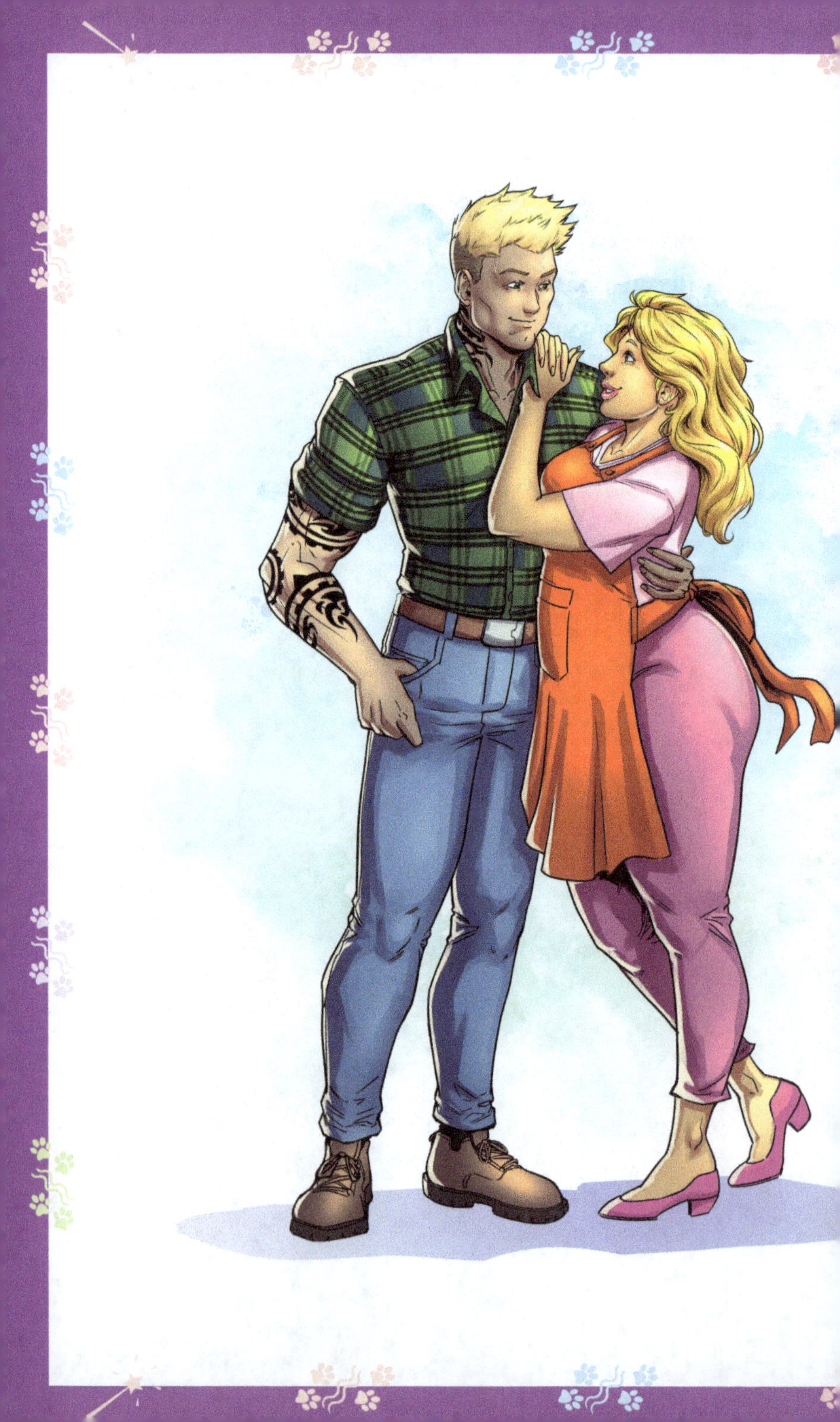

CHAPTER EIGHTEEN-BELLA

I WAS fast asleep on something hard and warm when my phone started ringing.

At first, I thought maybe I'd passed out on a sack of flour again—hey, it had happened before, don't judge—but no.

Flour didn't usually have a steady heartbeat or smell like pine needles, sunshine, and trouble.

I cracked one eye open, peeking at the situation.

Not my pink Egyptian cotton sheets with the ludicrously high thread count.

Nope. It was him.

Ermagerd.

Conrad Boman.

Bagged.

Tagged.

And sleeping in my bed like he owned the place.

Oh my Goddess. Did that really happen?

Judging from my slightly sore and profoundly happy girly bits, the answer was a resounding *hell yes.*

Yes, it did.

Usually, this was the part where I freaked out. Where I did the emotional equivalent of rolling myself into a cinnamon bun and hiding in the corner until the problem went away.

Happy afterglow or not, my track record with relationships was about as successful as a Gremlin running a water park.

Sure, I blamed society for giving curvy women a bad rap and making us feel like love came with a size restriction. But that wasn't the whole truth.

I'd been burned before.

Case in point: the last time I'd felt even a spark with a guy—*that turd Jameson.*

The man had a knack for making compliments feel like paper cuts.

"Go on a diet, Bella. Twenty pounds and you'd be so pretty."

"I'd love to take you to the carnival, but can you fit on that ride?"

"Instead of starting work at 4:30, can you make it 5:30? I hate it when you wake me up."

Yeah. Prince Charming material, right?

And because I was a younger, dumber version of myself back then, I'd let him chip away at me like I was a block of cheap marble, and he thought he was Michelangelo.

So I built walls.

Big ones.

With barbed wire.

And a moat.

And possibly a fire-breathing guard dragon.

But Conrad?

Conrad was *different*.

Even sleeping, the man was a walking advertisement for bad decisions wrapped in a good idea.

The way his big, warm body was curled around mine—like I was something precious, something worth keeping—made it almost impossible to remember why I'd sworn off "forever" in the first place.

And that was terrifying.

Because the last thing I wanted was to hand my heart to someone who could break it.

The phone rang again, but Conrad slept through

it like a professional cuddler who was paid by the hour.

His entire body was coiled around mine in a way that made me question both physics and human anatomy.

Arms locked holding me in place.

Legs tangled with mine.

Chest to my back.

And somehow his chin was hooked over my shoulder, all without cutting off my oxygen supply.

The man had Python skills even when he wasn't in scales.

Seriously, he was the best snuggler ever.

I flipping loved it.

So did certain parts of my anatomy, if the warm, tingly hum between my thighs meant anything.

The phone rang again.

Conrad didn't even twitch.

Whoever was calling was persistent, though.

Wiggling my booty (purely for the sake of escaping, not because I liked the friction, *probably*), I slithered across the big sexy beastie and snagged the phone.

"Hello?" I whispered.

"My Witchy, you must come. There was small fire—"

"Petyr! Oh no!"

My heart lurched.

Images of charred ovens and scorched lemon bars flashed in my head.

Blasted arsonist jerk wad.

Why was someone so intent on messing with me and my bakery?

"Hey, give me the phone, Love," Conrad murmured, his voice thick with sleep and something darker.

He plucked it from my frozen fingers like I was a toddler who couldn't be trusted with the good silverware.

"Petyr? Yeah, it's me. The boys are on their way. Is anyone hurt? Good. Got it. Yep, I have her."

Those last three words—*I have her*—hit me right in the sternum.

And in the gut.

And somewhere lower.

He had me.

Not just in the *wrapped around me like a human anaconda* way.

Not just physically.

No.

He had already managed to wedge himself into my heart when I wasn't looking.

Panic tried to creep in.

Before it could take root, I bolted out of bed—literally.

My legs got tangled in the sheets, and I gracelessly face-planted on the rug.

Conrad was there in a heartbeat, sliding down beside me, his expression somewhere between concerned boyfriend and man trying not to laugh his ass off.

His fingers brushed my hair back from my face before he cupped my cheeks, his touch warm and grounding.

"Don't borrow trouble, Bella," he murmured, that deep rumble settling right into my bones. "We'll figure everything out. Right now, clothes. We'll go to the bakery together. I've already alerted the boys. They replied that the fire was set in the dumpster this time. See? The bad guys couldn't get past your security."

Then he stood.

Naked.

My brain immediately supplied one word in neon letters,

MEGLADONG.

And because I am a mature, sophisticated woman, I stared.

Stared. Unblinkingly. For a very long time.

His semi-stiff trouser snake twitched under my gaze, as if it knew.

"Sssugar, if you don't stop looking at me like that," he growl-hissed, a sound that made my knees weak.

I shook my head like I could rattle my brain back into place.

"Right. Later. Clothes. Now. Let's get dressed."

"Right, we should hurry," he said, already grabbing my spare toothbrush and lining up next to me at the sink like we'd been doing this for years.

I had a *his-and-hers* vanity.

The *his* side was basically storage for my hair products.

But watching him brush his teeth there, I had a thought.

Maybe I could make room.

If I was very careful.

If I didn't let him see how much the idea warmed me.

Please, pretty please with cannoli cream on top, Goddess, do not let this man break my heart.

"I don't think the Goddess will mind," I muttered, and flicked my fingers, using a burst of pink-and-white sparkles to magic us both clean, dressed, and ready.

"Thanks, sweet Witch," Conrad grinned at his reflection.

I dressed him in jeans and a black t-shirt, both fresh and pressed. His skin was clean and healthy, and his hair shiny.

Even his boots gleamed like they'd just been polished.

"You look scrumptious," he said, then stole a quick, warm kiss before scooping me over his shoulder like I was nothing more than a bag of flour.

I squealed, but secretly?

Yeah, I liked it.

By the time we pulled up at the bakery in his pickup truck, the firetruck and the Sheriff's cruiser were already there.

Jaxson was questioning Petyr like he was a suspect on Law & Order: Supernatural Unit.

Gryn and Ivan were hovering nearby, their little magical auras bristling.

I barely noticed Conrad holding the door for me until he murmured, "Bella?"

Before I could answer, I was mobbed.

"Thank the Goddess you're alright!" Donny and

Evie chorused, tackling me in a two-pronged bestie hug.

"Yes, I'm fine!" I squeaked, muffled in Witch boobage. "What are you two even doing here?"

Evie pulled back with a guilty grin. "Well, I almost didn't come. I heard *dumpster fire* and thought maybe it was a metaphor for your love life."

"Ha ha," I said flatly, but couldn't stop the smile tugging at my lips.

Donny raised a brow and glanced at Conrad, then back at me.

"Judging by the way your hair's mussed and your lipstick's MIA, I'd say it's not a total disaster."

"Shut. Up." I hissed.

But yeah, maybe they weren't wrong.

CHAPTER NINETEEN-CONRAD

LAST NIGHT WAS the best night of my life to date, hands down.

Sleeping curled around my sweet Bella? It was heaven on earth.

But all that post-coital bliss and my plans for waking her up with my head between her warm, think thighs faded the second I heard that phone ring.

My sexy little Witch slid off my body, trying to be stealthy, but I was so attuned to her I was alert and ready before she even noticed.

I tried not to let rage and anger take over, but when I saw the smoke curling over the bakery roof? Something primal in me snapped.

Not the calm, calculated awareness of a predator. No.

This was the mate part of me—*the beast in my blood*—rising up, ready to burn down the whole damn world if it meant keeping Bella safe.

"Oh, oh no," she murmured softly.

And the second I saw her—pink Crocs, hair mussed, eyes wide with worry—my Python uncoiled inside me, pushing for control.

It wanted to wrap around her, shield her, make damn sure no one and nothing could ever hurt her again.

"Stay behind me, Sugar," I murmured, but she was already pushing forward toward the yellow tape, toward the fire crew and Petyr.

My girl didn't understand—when I said stay behind me, I meant let me take every hit for you until I'm dust.

I caught up in two strides, slipping my hand into hers.

She didn't pull away.

Good.

Maybe she was starting to get it.

Maybe she was beginning to understand what she meant to me.

It soothed my beast a little. But the truth was I'd never be okay with her so close to danger.

"My Witchy! There you are!" Petyr's voice carried over the crowd.

He looked tense, a streak of soot across his temple, but otherwise fine.

My muscles loosened a notch. I knew if there was still a lingering threat, her Domovyk familiar wouldn't be so calm.

"What happened?" Bella asked, rushing to him.

"Small fire in dumpster only. Damage is minimal. No injuries," he assured her.

His eyes cut to me, sharp and assessing, like he knew exactly what was going through my head.

And he probably did.

The man might not be a Shifter, but he was family to her.

Which meant this moment mattered.

"I'll be doubling patrols until this bastard is caught," I told him, my voice like gravel.

"Conrad, you can't—"

I narrowed my eyes, and kept right on talking.

"She's not walking anywhere alone. Not at night. Not even across the damn street."

Bella opened her mouth, probably to tell me I was being overbearing, but I kept going, loud enough for everyone in the parking lot to hear—Jax, Ryan, the Sheriff, half the fire crew.

Hell, even the damn Domovyks had gone silent.

"Bella Strega, you're mine, and I protect what's mine," I said, my voice carrying over the hiss of the hoses.

"Does everyone hear me? I don't care how long it takes her to say yes to my claim or accept that we are bonded, bite or not, but this little Witch is still mine. And I'm putting everyone on notice. Everyone in the whole damn town. This is going to stop! I *will* protect her with everything I have until my last breath, and if anyone here has a problem with that, they can step the hell up now."

Bella froze, those big eyes snapping to mine.

Yeah, Sugar, I meant every damn word.

Petyr didn't blink.

Didn't flinch.

Then, slowly, he smiled. It was a knowing, almost smug smile—the kind a man gives when he's been waiting for someone to finally grow the balls to say what needed saying.

"Then you have my blessing, Python," he said, clapping a broad hand on my shoulder. "She is stubborn, but she is worth it."

The crowd murmured, a ripple of amusement and approval passing through them.

Bella's cheeks flushed pink, but she didn't run.

Didn't deny it.

Didn't tell me to shut up.

And for now, that was good enough.

Then, she stepped closer, her arm brushing mine, and whispered, "You're impossible."

"Damn right," I murmured back, dropping my head so only she could hear the next part. "But I'm yours, sweet Witch. Always."

And as far as I was concerned, that was the end of it.

The town knew.

Her people knew.

Now it was just a matter of time before she admitted what I already knew in my bones—Maribella Strega was mine.

Not in the casual, oh yeah, we've been seeing each other way.

No. This was bone-deep. Blood-deep. Mate-deep.

The Python in me already recognized her, claimed her, marked her in ways she probably didn't even realize yet.

And the man in me? Yeah, he was just as far gone.

If anyone so much as breathed wrong in her direction, I'd be right there. Slaying Demons, fighting Dragons, wrestling rogue Shifters into the dirt—*hell, I'd even sit through a Warlock HOA meeting if it meant keeping her safe.*

And it wasn't just because my Python was that freaking awesome—though, for the record, he was.

It was because this woman, hell, she owned me. Entirely.

She had my Python.

My fealty.

My loyalty.

My heart, mind, body, and soul.

All of it.

Maribella didn't just sneak under my skin—she built a damn condo there and hung curtains.

She was in my blood now, in every beat of my heart, in every instinct that told me I'd be less than a man without her.

There was nothing I wouldn't do to ensure her safety.

My sweet Witch had the biggest heart. And I vowed to keep it safe—*no matter what.*

I'd already made peace with the fact that I'd kill for her.

But more importantly, I'd live for her.

Every sunrise, every laugh, every cinnamon-sugar kiss—*yeah, those were mine to protect.*

She just didn't know yet that forever wasn't a question.

It was already decided.

CHAPTER TWENTY-BELLA

THAT EVIE and Donny were waiting when we pulled up warmed something inside me I didn't even realize had been going cold.

Truth was, I'd been feeling a little glum about our friendship lately.

Ever since we'd discovered Grandpa Al was our grandpa—like *all* of our grandfather—I'd been doing this weird internal shuffle, trying to figure out where I fit in the picture.

Like maybe I was the odd puzzle piece that got left in the couch cushions and only got found years later.

"Of course we are here! We're besties. And cousins! And we've been really worried about you with all this craziness going on. I had no idea it was still going on. How could you keep it from us?" Donny snapped.

"I'm always around. I talk to you guys every day," I defended myself lamely.

"Yeah, right. You've been so closed off lately. I'm serious, Bella, we've been trying to get you to open up for weeks," Evie mock-scolded, her voice wobbling just enough that I could hear the emotion under the sass.

Her big eyes shimmered with unshed tears, and I knew one sniffle from Donny and I'd be toast.

Full-on, sobbing, ugly cry toast.

"What are you two talking about?" I tried to play it casual, but my voice cracked right at the end.

"She's right, you know. We have been really worried, *Hells Bells*," Donny said, using the nickname she'd called me since our schoolgirl days.

She twirled the end of my ponytail around her finger, smiling just a little too softly for my comfort.

"About what, though? I'm fine—"

"Fine?" Evie's brows shot up. "This is the *fourth* time someone has attacked your store, and I had to hear about it from Jaxson, Bella! What the heck?"

"No way, I told you guys about this—" I started, then paused.

Okay, maybe I'd mentioned it in passing, once or twice, but yeah.

They were right.

I'd been playing my cards close, trying not to dump my drama on anyone else's doorstep.

Before the guilt could chew a hole in my stomach, Conrad's warm hand rubbed my shoulder.

He leaned down, brushed a kiss across my cheek like it was the most natural thing in the world, and said, "I'll give you girls some privacy, but I'll be right over there, Sugar."

He gave the girls a nod before striding over to where Jaxson and Ryan were standing.

Ryan was chugging a bottle of water, soot on his nose, the faint scent of charred garbage wafting off him.

Poor guy.

Shifter noses made that at least ten times worse.

"Oh, wow, that stinks," I muttered.

"I'm on it," Donny said.

She gave me one last squeeze and strutted toward the mess like she was about to audition for *Witches Who Clean, Season One.*

With a few graceful movements and a little muttered magic, she had the dumpster *spotless.*

Sparkling.

Like it belonged in a fancy downtown coffee shop instead of behind my bakery.

And there I'd been, doing everything by hand like a chump, when all I needed was my friends.

"How come *friend* can do magic?" Petyr's voice came out of nowhere, making me jump.

"Oh, that's 'cause the personal gain foul only happens when you use magic selfishly. Donny's helping Bella out, so it's all good," Evie explained with a small smile.

"Da, makes sense. Oh, I found this by the dumpster, my Witchy."

Petyr held up an empty tuna can and a pile of old scratch-offs like they were rare artifacts.

"Why is someone eating fish and gambling behind my business?"

"Yeah, is there a secret alleyway bingo club I don't know about? You know, I'm the mayor, and I'm pretty sure you need a permit for that," Evie added.

"Okay, something is going on in Castor's Corner," I murmured. "Something weird."

"Well, weirder than usual. Especially if it involves tuna," Evie said, grabbing the can and sniffing it. *Gross.*

I was still frowning and tapping my chin when

Evie's stomach let out a growl loud enough to make the local crows take off. Her cheeks turned bright pink.

"Let's go inside," I said, plucking the garbage from her hands and tossing it in the dumpster. "It's almost time for me to start my day anyway, and I'll make you all some fresh donuts."

"Thank *gawd*," Donny moaned, rushing towards us, and Evie clapped like she'd just won the jackpot.

We waved at the boys, knowing they'd heard us and would come in once they wrapped up.

Inside, our familiars joined the cozy chaos, and within twenty minutes, I had the first batch of fried goodness cooling on the racks.

I headed to the walk-in fridge and pantry, hauling out today's flavor lineup.

"Ooh, what are you making today, Bella?" Evie asked, rubbing her tummy with theatrical flair.

I shot Donny a look over my shoulder—Evie was acting squirrelly.

Like, extra squirrelly.

Donny just shrugged, her newly blonde hair bouncing, which told me even she didn't know what was going on.

"You'll see," I said, flipping the donuts before heading back to prep toppings.

Donny took over tea duty while Evie stared at the counter like she was mentally marrying each topping.

I'd pulled ingredients for *Hazelnut Chocolate Heaven*, *Candied Apple Pie*, *Bananas Foster* (yes, with my new extract), and, of course, *Lemon Meringue Logs*.

"Ooh, can I make a special request?" Evie asked just as the boys came in.

"Sure," I said, already bracing myself.

And then she hit me with it—*maple frosting, spinach stuffing, bacon crumbles, jalapeños, candied apple sprinkles, and peanut butter.*

By the time she finished, half the room looked green, even the boys who'd just joined us.

Jaxson actually dry heaved.

"Um, I guess."

I wiggled my fingers, magic swirling, and produced the monstrosity she'd requested inside a piping bag.

Petyr slapped a skull-and-crossbones sticker on it, and we high-fived like a couple of middle-school pranksters.

"You're really going to eat this?" I asked, sliding the donuts over to her.

"Hell yeah!" Evie spoke with the conviction of a woman on a mission.

"Jaxson? Oh, Jaxson?" I sing-songed.

"Yes, Bella?" the big-bad Wolf asked warily.

"I think you better have a talk with my cousin here, and the sooner the better. Don't you?"

Donny was doubled over laughing, and Ryan wasn't doing much better.

He kissed Donny goodbye, snagged a bag of cinnamon sugar donuts for the firehouse, and promised to be back later.

"You know these are amazing, right?" Conrad said, stealing my attention—*and two Lemon Meringue Logs.*

Which is exactly when Evie launched herself over the counter, stole the pastry bag, and started slurping down the nightmare filling like it was a delicacy.

A wrestling match ensued, Jaxson trying and failing to wrestle it away without getting jalapeño-peanut butter goop all over himself.

"*Ohmygawd, Evie! No!*" Donny wailed, but Evie was too far gone.

Lucky Jaxson.

Eww.

Also TMI.

CHAPTER TWENTY-ONE-BELLA

AFTER CLEANING up Evie's mess, I'd gone into autopilot.

Feed people, that's what I did.

That's what kept my hands moving and my brain from spinning out into the kind of places where I started questioning my life choices and relationships.

I managed to whip up a few goodies for the rest of us, plus a pot of tea and coffee for whoever wanted some—*which, naturally, was everyone.*

Feeding people was my love language, and I adored it when something I created made someone sigh and smile.

Safe. Predictable. Normal.

That was my lane.

I shook my head and sipped my tea, pushing the last half of my Bananas Foster donut across the plate toward my, well, *I guess he was my boyfriend.*

"Damn straight I'm your boyfriend," Conrad growl-hissed against my lips, licking a smidge of cream I hadn't realized was smeared on my cheek.

The man licked me.

Like I was both dessert and main course.

And my body?

Yeah, my body was absolutely here for it, tingles zipping down my spine, my magic doing that fizzy champagne-bubble thing it always did around him.

I took another bite, trying to regain some dignity, and—*oh, fabulous*—more cream.

This time it smeared across the corner of my mouth.

My giggles betrayed me before I could wipe it away, and Conrad just took my face in those big, gentle hands and kissed me clean.

Slow. Sweet. Intimate.

Oh, great.

Now my whole face probably looked like I'd been making out with a Bear who'd been in the custard jar.

I must look ridiculous.

Just a chubby Witch eating custard and making a mess of myself.

"Not to me, beautiful Bella."

His voice went low and dangerous, his emerald eyes locking on mine.

"For the record, you have the perfect body, and watching you eat is like my favorite kind of porn, sweet Witch."

My mouth dropped open.

Did he just—?

Was that—?

No. No no no no no.

This wasn't supposed to happen.

We were taking things slow.

We'd made a deal.

No mate-bond rush.

No losing myself before I was ready.

He said he was okay with it.

"At your pace, Sugar. I swear," he rumbled, but there was a nervous edge to his voice.

His pupils narrowed, his tongue flicking like he was tasting my magic in the air.

My stomach dropped.

My chest went tight.

"What is it, Sugar?" he asked, brows furrowing

like he could read every thought I was desperately trying to shove back into a locked vault.

And then—*oh Goddess*—his eyes widened.

Oh. Hell. No.

"Are you reading my mind?" I yelped.

Zap.

A mini mountain of hardtack exploded from my fingertips, raining down across the counter in a loud pitter-patter of magic-induced carbohydrate panic.

The smell of toasted flour and overbaked crackers filled the room like some kind of weird bakery crime scene.

My heart was racing so fast I thought it might just blast out of my ribcage, slap him across the face, and run off into the night without me.

I didn't know whether I wanted to cry, kiss him, or shove him into the nearest bread oven.

Because this bond—*this thing between us*—it was happening without my permission.

Without me being ready.

And that felt like betrayal.

Betrayal by him for pushing too hard.

Betrayal by my own magic for answering him so easily.

Betrayal by my traitorous heart for wanting him anyway.

My emotions were all over the place, and my magic—*oh, my magic*—was just feeding off it, sparking along my skin, jittering like a hyper-caffeinated squirrel.

If I didn't calm down soon, there'd be exploding pastries, and trust me, that was never as fun as it sounded.

Donny jumped.

Evie squeaked.

And I just stood there glaring at him like *how dare you mind-snoop me after what we agreed on.*

"Um. Ooopsss," he whisper-hissed.

I kicked the crackers aside and turned on the man whose head had been buried between my thighs for the better part of two hours last night.

The nerve.

This was why I didn't do relationships.

Because men couldn't be trusted to respect boundaries.

Especially stupid sexy Snake men!

"Bella—"

"Uh-uh!" I jabbed a finger into his chest hard enough to make him sway back a step. "I told you—*no mating!* We are supposed to be *going out.* Keeping it light. That was the deal!"

"I can't help it, Bella. You're mine!" His voice was low, almost pleading.

"Sugar. please, try to understand. I'm trying to go slow for your sake, but I'm a Shifter. The matebond is already there. Surely you can feel it. You have to know how I feel about you."

"Well, you already freaking announced it, but I thought that was just posturing!"

The worry in his eyes hit me like a cold wave.

He wasn't angry.

He was scared.

Of what?

Of losing you, a voice sounded inside my head.

And that was the problem.

I didn't know how to carry someone else's feelings without dropping them. I barely managed my own without making a mess.

What happened when he decided I wasn't enough?

Or when he decided he wanted to change me?

Nobody outside of family and my girls had ever loved me as-is.

No edits.

No *if you'd just do this* clauses.

No man had ever looked at me the way he did.

I had no map for this.

But it was all too fast, and I felt slightly betrayed at his going ahead and forming a bond with me without my knowledge or approval.

"That's it. I need you to leave."

His jaw worked, muscles tightening like he was holding back a thousand words.

"Please, Bella. Just hear me out."

"I can't. Not right now. Just go."

"Come on, bro. Let's give them some time," Jaxson muttered from behind him, and I heard more than saw them leave.

The moment Conrad was gone, it felt like someone had ripped out a piece of my soul and taken it with him.

I sank onto one of the stools behind the counter and let the tears fall.

In seconds, there were arms around me—one smelling suspiciously like spinach and peanut butter (thanks, Evie)—and the three of us just sat there and cried.

Messy, hiccuppy, not-pretty tears.

"Why my Witchy cries?!" Petyr's voice rang out a moment later. "I will destroy Shifter who did this!"

I glanced over to see him already chewing a fistful of hardtack like it was gourmet.

How the little gremlin could stomach it, I had no idea.

But hey—free cleanup crew.

"Oh, no. Petyr, I think maybe Bella is just having some feelings," Evie tried to reason with my familiar.

I could have saved her the trouble. He was like a dog with a bone when it came to some things. Me crying was one of them.

"No! My Witch cries. The Snake dies!"

Then—*zap!* A jolt of magic zipped through the air leaving the three of us sneezing for thirty seconds after.

"Bella, you need to call him back—achoo!" Evie sneezed.

"What?" I sniffled, sitting up.

Too late—*Petyr was gone.*

"Uh-oh," Donny murmured, swiping under her eyes with her sleeve. "I better tell Ryan to let Conrad know."

"Don't let that Snake know anything!" I barked, but my voice cracked halfway through.

"Honey," Donny said, fixing me with her listen to Auntie Donny face, "your Domovyk is about to try and cut his ball sack off. Now, I know you're mad at him but trust me—you want that ball sack right where it is."

I gaped, then slumped.

"You're right. Call him."

"Honey?" Evie said, giving me that cautious tone people use when approaching a feral cat. "Can you tell us what just happened? We thought maybe it was a rocky start, but why are you fighting with your mate?"

"Will everyone please stop saying that? He is not my mate!"

The two of them exchanged a look—*eyebrows up, lips pursed*—and then the heifers started laughing.

"What is so funny?" I demanded, heat rushing up my neck.

"You," Donny gasped between cackles. "You keep saying *'he's not my mate'* but it's written all over your face, *Hells Bells*. You've got it bad."

"She's glowing," Evie added helpfully. "Like, legit magical glow. You look like a lightning bug in love."

"I do not glow!" I said, horrified.

"Uh-huh," they chorused, smirking. "Sure you don't."

CHAPTER TWENTY-TWO-BELLA

AT THE TASTY *Tart*

"Oh, honey, of course he is your mate."

Donny snorted.

Evie rolled her eyes like I'd just told her water wasn't wet.

And Petyr, he growled from over in the corner.

"That very first night, I saw the two of you together and I know you felt it too. Hell, me, and Jaxson did too. I was just fighting it. But I thought you were smarter than me, Bella," Evie said, patting me with the hand that was *thankfully* not covered in her *special donut filling.*

"You, wait, you think I'm smarter than you?" I blinked at her, floored.

Look—I'm blonde.

I can bake like a goddess, and I can charm a soufflé into rising with my voice alone.

But book smart like Evie? Not exactly my lane.

Don't get me wrong, I'm not mouth-breather dumb, and Donny is quick as a whip.

But I always thought Evie had the big-brain energy in this trio.

"When it comes to a lot of things, actually," she said, as if she hadn't just dropped that truth bomb into my lap.

"Seriously, Bella," Donny cut in, leaning over the counter with a cat-that-ate-the-canary grin. "I thought you and Conrad had hooked up months ago."

"Well, funny story," I hedged, avoiding their eyes as heat climbed up my neck. "We kinda did hook up right away."

"AHHHH! YOU ARE SUCH A SLUT!" Evie squealed with delight.

"Way to go, girl!" Donny crowed.

And then they *pounced.*

Two giggling, squealing, cupcake-scented tornadoes of affection.

I twisted away from their tickling fingers, narrowly dodged the buttercream blob Donny tried to swipe across my nose, and the three of us ended up in a pile on the floor, breathless from laughter.

"Oh my Goddess, I need to go on a diet," Evie wheezed.

"About that," Donny started, but I pinched her arm.

Not our secret to tell—especially not when it most definitely involved a certain Wolf Shifter she was mated to.

"Oh my Goddess, I've been such a jerk about this, haven't I?"

"I don't know about being a jerk, Bells, but you sure are giving Conrad a run for his money," Evie said.

"Hey, he's a Shifter. They have wonderful stamina. Now how about we tackle this mess? I've got heads waiting for me at the salon," Donny said.

With a bit of wandless magic and a flick of all our wrists, we cleaned up the chaos.

Which, frankly, made me feel a little guilty for how long I'd been doing every post-baking cleanup solo.

"So, you really hooked up like way back when," Donny prompted, wiggling her fingers for more gossip.

"Yes, we hooked up," I admitted, then sighed. "But

you know what happened last time I had a man—I just don't want a repeat."

"You are NOT talking about that turd, Jameson Vorhees, are you?" Evie's eyes narrowed like she was about to hex someone into the next county.

"Actually—"

"Bella!" they chorused, scandalized.

"Okay, Maribella Strega, I take that back about you being smart," Evie declared, swatting my butt.

"Hey! I'm like the Scarecrow after he gets his brain! You can't just *take it back* now," I protested.

"Fine," Evie huffed. "But you should know—Jameson Vorhees was a complete two-timing creep, and he did not deserve you."

"He said he left because I wouldn't change for him," I mumbled.

"What? That is a complete lie!" Donny's nose wrinkled. "Should we tell her?"

"Tell me what?"

"Bella, Jameson Vorhees came on to both of us countless times while you were dating him," Evie said flatly. "Finally, he got the hint we were *never* going to betray you."

I froze.

"It's true," Donny added. "And later, we found out he was dating Misty Palmer at the same time. And

Misty's Uncle Montgomery threatened to have his powers drained and his Warlock World Coven membership revoked if he didn't leave town immediately—"

"Wait. What? He left because he was juggling *two Witches* and got caught?"

"Two that we know of. Yup," Evie said.

"Oh Goddess, she hates us now," Donny groaned. "Look, we didn't tell you because we didn't find out about Misty until six months later, and you seemed fine by then."

"He told me I was fat," I said, the words tasting like ash.

"What?" they snarled in unison, aqua and gold sparks dancing at their fingertips.

"Not in here, ladies," I warned. "Anyway, he told me I was too big for a man of his standing to be seen with. Said things like if I loved him, I'd glamor myself while I worked on losing weight. I refused."

"How dare he!" Evie's voice cracked with outrage.

"That Warlock piece of shi—" Donny started but was cut off by Petyr strolling in like he hadn't just dropped off the face of the earth.

He looked rumpled, a little singed, and smug as a cat with cream.

"I have avenged your virtue, my Witchy, and I

have given permission to the Shifter to court one as yourself—but only if you wish."

"You did *what*?" I asked, torn between laughter and alarm.

"Where I am from, fathers of daughters defend. Your father is not here—so I step in. Snake Shifter has proven to be a good man. His heart is true. But still, it is you who must decide. Now, I go back to dumpster to sniff out arson."

"Uh, okay. Thanks?" I mumbled, wide-eyed as my familiar continued on his way.

"Wow," Evie breathed. "That was so beautiful!"

"Oh great, she's crying again," Donny muttered, hugging her.

"So, Bella, are you mad at us?" Evie asked, tears running into her mouth.

I handed her a tissue.

"What? No! I love you girls. We're besties and cousins, but I admit, I've missed you. Watching you both get close to your mates has made me kind of afraid, you know."

"We will never abandon you," Donny said firmly.

"And you don't have to worry about being alone," Evie sniffled. "You have Conrad too. That Snake *loves* you. I can feeeeel it."

Then, she growled.

Actually growled.

"Oh dear Goddess," I muttered, ushering them toward the back. "Get her home before she scares off my customers. And tell Jaxson to get his tail home and give his mate the news she needs to hear."

"But I wanted to talk about the wedding cake!" Donny called as I shut the door.

"Too bad. It's my gift, I have full creative control!" I hollered back.

Then I just stood there.

For a full minute, letting the truth sink in.

There was nothing wrong with me.

I didn't *drive* a man away because I couldn't keep him.

Jameson Vorhees was a lying, cheating, power-hungry Warlock. Period.

And Conrad Boman?

He was nothing like that.

Patient. Steady. Kind.

And maybe—*if I asked nicely*—Conrad would be *mine*.

Before I could lose my nerve, I grabbed my phone and texted him:

BELLA

I think we should talk, Big Guy.

His reply came instantly.

SNAKE MAN

Just tell me when and where, Sugar.

BELLA

You pick. I'll be finished at six.

SNAKE MAN

I'll be there, Sugar.

My heart pounded like a drum.

I wished I had time to shop for something slinky and spellbinding, but he'd have to take me as I was— *Witchy flour smudges and all.*

The bakery mystery still loomed large, but maybe that was the point—two heads (one belonging to a very large Python Shifter) were better than one.

After years of dodging commitment, I was about to dive headfirst into it.

Here goes nothing.

CHAPTER TWENTY-THREE-
CONRAD

MY PYTHON HAD BEEN TRYING to tear me to shreds all damn day after I'd fucked up royally with my sweet Witch.

Every flicker of her magic I'd caught on the edge of my senses was like an itch I couldn't scratch—*tantalizing, teasing, reminding me exactly what I'd lost when she'd told me to take a walk.*

But ever since she texted me—*I think we should talk, snake man.*

My beast had been losing his scaly little mind.

Coiling.

Stretching.

Hissing like we were on the verge of a fight.

Except this wasn't fight-energy—it was *want-her-now-or-I'll-shred-you-from-the-inside* energy.

I'd never intended to form a matebond without her permission. Hell, I'd promised her *slow*. I'd meant it.

But the Fates?

Those tricky, meddling, sadistic puppet masters?

They didn't give a damn about permission.

They just snapped their cosmic fingers, tangled two souls together, and walked away like they hadn't just lit someone's life on fire.

Now, I was grateful to those all-powerful beings for gifting me with Maribella Strega.

Grateful, worshipful, the whole nine yards.

But come on—give a guy a chance to *woo* his woman.

Let me buy her flowers, cook her dinner, save her from a dumpster fire or two before throwing us into the deep end.

How was I supposed to court her properly *and* protect her if the bond kept tightening every time we so much as breathed in the same zip code?

I was starting to understand those old Shifter tales of mate raids back in the Viking and Clan days.

Find her.

Claim her.

Mark her so deep she couldn't even think about another male without her body turning traitor.

If I could, I'd hoist my Sugar over my shoulder, carry her to my lair, and keep her there until she was so high on me she forgot her own name.

Might be cheating a bit, but a Snake had to do what a Snake had to do.

Luckily, my girl texted me before I could go completely unhinged and start drawing up blueprints for a romantic kidnapping.

Not ruling it out for later.

Just seeing how this goes first.

When she opened the bakery's side door, flour-dusted and perfect in black capris and a pink top that clung to her curves like it had been sewn there by the Goddess herself, my Python went still.

Alert. Ready.

Possessive to the point my jaw ached from keeping my fangs sheathed.

And I swear to all the Old Gods and the New—if she'd told me to strip naked and slither through broken glass just to be near her, I'd have been halfway down the hallway already.

Instead, I kept my hands shoved in my jeans pockets, because one look at her soft, wary eyes told me I was already on thin ice.

"Hey, Sugar," I said low, the word tasting like a promise.

She stepped aside.

"Come in. I got home a little while ago, but I made coffee."

I would've drunk molten tar if she'd said it with that careful little voice.

Her place smelled like cinnamon and fresh bread. *Safe. Home.*

My inner Python uncoiled, wanting to wrap her up until the rest of the damn world stopped existing.

I sat at her kitchen table, but my gaze followed her every move—how her ponytail swung when she poured the coffee, the way she bit her lip when she set my mug down like we were on opposite ends of some negotiation.

She sat across from me.

"So, I hear Petyr gave you his blessing to, um, *court me.*"

A chuckle rumbled from my chest.

"Yeah. Nearly broke my nose in the process, but I took it as a win."

Her mouth twitched.

Half a smile, half a warning.

"You know I've been trying to come to a decision about us, and I know it's been taking a while."

I leaned forward, resting my forearms on the table, voice low enough that it was just for her.

"You take all the time you need, Sugar. But here's something you can't decide and it's this, Bella, I'm not going anywhere."

"But what if—"

"No what ifs, Sugar. But how about we start small, okay? So, let's just say I'm not going anywhere until whoever's been targeting your bakery is caught. Not until you know, without a doubt, that I've got you. And not until you look me in the eye and tell me you don't want me."

Her breath hitched. She didn't look away.

Didn't tell me to leave again, and damn, I was glad for that.

The Python in me surged, the need to claim her coiling tight in my gut.

But she was human enough to be wary, Witch enough to fight me on instinct.

So I held the line. For now.

"Why?" she whispered. "Why me?"

That broke something open in my chest.

"Because I've been walking this earth a long damn time, Sugar. And no one—*no one*—has ever felt like home until you. You don't change for me. You don't shrink yourself. You burn brighter. And I'd fight every bastard in Castor's Corner and beyond to keep it that way."

Her fingers toyed with the handle of her mug, the pink in her cheeks deepening.

I knew then—*pressure or not, arson or not*—she wanted me here.

Which was perfect.

Because I wasn't about to let her handle any of this alone.

I pulled a folder from my jacket and slid it across the table.

"Security cam stills. I've been tracking patterns—times, nights, even wind direction. Whoever's behind this isn't random. They've been watching you."

Her brows drew together. "You've been keeping records?"

"Every move they've made," I said. "And every move you've made since the night we met."

Her lips parted like she wanted to scold me, but the flush on her throat told me she wasn't exactly put off by the idea.

"I protect what's mine, Bella," I told her simply. "And you are mine. Whether you admit it yet or not."

She stared at me for a long beat before her gaze dropped to the stills.

Then she sighed, shaking her head and fighting a grin.

"Two heads are better than one."

The smile that pulled at my mouth was slow, certain.

"Damn right, Sugar."

I reached across the table, took her hand, and didn't let go.

Tonight, we'd talk strategy.

Tomorrow, we'd hunt.

And when this was over, she'd never doubt who she belonged to again.

But first.

I stood up and moved in close, close enough that the scent of her—*warm sugar and fried dough with that hint of magic*—wrapped around me like a spell I had no interest in breaking.

I took her hand and pulled her to her feet, so she was right there in front of me.

Sweet. Soft. Irresistible.

"I know you wanna take things slow, so I'm asking, should I stay, or do you want me to go?"

She blinked at me, that perfect pink mouth parting just slightly.

My hands itched to cup her face, but I kept them loose at my sides.

She was a skittish creature sometimes, my Bella

—like a stray cat who wanted to be petted but wasn't quite sure if the hand was safe yet.

Her gaze darted away, then back to mine.

"You'd really go if I said so?"

"If you told me to." My voice came out rougher than I meant it to. "But you should know, I'd take my sweet damn time walking out that door."

That earned me a little huff of laughter, and her shoulders relaxed. "You're impossible."

"No. I'm stubborn. And I'm yours."

She swallowed, and that little flicker of doubt I'd been sensing from her—*those walls she kept between us*—wavered.

The kitchen smelled of cinnamon and coffee, the hiss and pop of the kettle settling down whispered in the air.

But all I could hear was her breathing. All I could smell was her sweet citrus scent.

She was everything. Everywhere.

I couldn't help myself.

I reached out, brushed my knuckles down her cheek, slow enough she could lean away if she wanted.

She didn't.

Thank the Goddess, she leaned into it.

"You've had enough people in your life walk

away when things got complicated," I murmured. "I'm not one of them. So unless you shove me out that door, Bella, I'm staying. I'm protecting you. And I'm going to keep proving to you that you're it for me. My mate. My Witch."

Her eyes shimmered—*dammit, was that a tear?*—but then she did the most Bella thing ever.

She sniffed, squared her shoulders, and muttered, "You're lucky you're hot."

That broke me.

I laughed, low and relieved, and before she could come up with another smart-ass comment, I was kissing her.

Slow at first.

Testing.

My lips on hers, the faint taste of sugar and that last bite of Bananas Foster donut we'd shared earlier still lingering.

She sighed into me, her hands fisting in the front of my shirt, and just like that, the dam broke.

I pulled her against me, deepening the kiss, my tongue sliding against hers in a slow, claiming stroke.

Something popped somewhere behind us, but nothing in this world could've made me move.

Her magic prickled over my skin, little jolts of

heat and light, as if her body was saying yes, yes, yes even if her stubborn brain wasn't ready to admit it.

I backed her toward the counter, lifting her effortlessly to sit on the edge.

She wrapped her legs around my waist without hesitation, and I felt her melt against me.

"Conrad," she whispered, her voice a mix of warning and want.

"I've got you, Bella." I dragged my lips down her jaw, tasting the soft skin at her throat, breathing her in.

"Not going anywhere."

Her head tipped back, giving me access, and my self-control frayed another inch.

My hands slid under her shirt, palms memorizing every inch of warm, soft skin.

She gasped when my thumbs brushed the underside of her breasts, arching into me.

"Just let me lock the door," she whispered.

Her magic surged, a quick shimmer of power sealing us in.

The entire house hissed, and the walls hummed with energy.

In here, it was just us.

I came back to her mouth, kissing her hard this

time, pouring every ounce of want and promise into it.

Her fingers tangled in my hair, nails scraping lightly against my scalp, and a low growl rumbled out of me.

Clothes went fast after that—*her shirt over her head, my belt unbuckled, her leggings tugged down with a breathless laugh.*

I slid my hands over her hips, pulling her to the very edge of the counter.

She was flushed, eyes bright with magic and need, and I knew I'd never get enough of her.

"Tell me to stop," I murmured against her lips, even though I prayed she wouldn't.

She shook her head, pulling me closer.

"Don't you dare."

That was all the permission I needed.

I slammed my lips to hers, right there in the warm, sugar-scented heart of her home.

My fingers gripped her thick thighs, and I pressed her knees wide, fitting my eager cock to her dripping entrance.

"Mine," I hissed, thrusting my hips and pressing deep inside of her heated body.

So wet. So warm.

Her soft moans mixing with the hum of the earth.

Every touch, every kiss, was a promise—*one I had no intention of ever breaking.*

By the time we finally stilled, breathless and clinging to each other, the oven timer dinged.

Bella laughed against my chest. "Guess the muffins are done."

"Let them wait," I murmured, kissing her hair. "I can't, Sugar. I need you again, now."

"Then take me, Conrad. Take me, please."

How could I turn down such an offer?

The answer was easy. I couldn't.

And I never would.

CHAPTER TWENTY-FOUR- BELLA

THE FOLLOWING MORNING

I was already mentally running through the day's muffin and tart lineup, wondering if Mira had beaten me in and gotten the ovens preheated and the fryers going.

My brain was still doing a happy little jitterbug over the perfect batter recipe that had popped into my head during that dreamy, half-asleep moment right before wakefulness.

You know, the magical space where genius ideas are born—*like chocolate-covered potato chips or putting your ex's cursed mirror on eBay.*

And okay, fine.

It wasn't just my culinary brilliance that sealed the deal.

The real inspiration?

A certain sly, sultry, shower-singing Snake man with a voice like sin dipped in honey.

Conrad's morning serenade had been distracting. *Deliciously distracting.*

The kind of distracting that made me want to slather myself in whipped cream and see if he could hit the high notes.

But it wasn't all him.

The other guilty party was the rhinestone-jump-suit-wearing King of Rock himself.

Elvis, you magnificent hunka-hunka-burnin' genius.

Somehow—don't ask me how—Snake Man plus Elvis had birthed the idea for my new *Peanut Butter Bacon Donut Delights.*

And wouldn't you know it? When I let it slip in the Tasty Tart's socials that my new flavor would be featured in today's specials—the townies flipped.

They were bound to be the new obsession of everyone in Castor's Corner.

Even Mr. Dorian, who usually acted like I personally offended his ancestors every time he came into the bakery, had pre-ordered a dozen.

On a scale of one to ten, these babies were an eleven.

Conceited? Nah.

Confident? Absolutely.

False modesty will get you nowhere in life—Granny drilled that into me so hard I was surprised it didn't appear in my Book of Shadows.

I was a fine baker.

No—scratch that.

I was a damn fine baker.

And if the Goddess herself descended from on high to try my Donut Delights, I'd probably get a celestial thumbs-up, and maybe a divine request for a dozen more.

But even better than having a brand new donut idea was how I felt today.

No doubting myself. *Or him.*

No regrets about last night at all, actually.

See, now that the hole in my heart I hadn't even realized I was lugging around had been sneakily filled to bursting, my baking had taken on a life of its own.

Yeah, yeah, I'd been holding out on myself.

Too stubborn and too scared to admit that maybe —*just maybe*—my smexy pants Snake Shifter, Conrad, wasn't the same as the walking dumpster fires I'd dated before.

He wasn't some Jameson-Vorhees-type Warlockwannabe with commitment issues and a personality like burnt toast.

Conrad was his own man.

And me? I wasn't some naïve Kitchen Witch's apprentice anymore.

I was Bella Strega, Kitchen Witch extraordinaire, with a thriving business, friends who loved me, and a sexy Python who made me see stars.

Conrad wasn't trying to change me or own me.

He just wanted to be with me.

And I was about ninety-nine point nine and a half percent certain I wanted that, too.

Okay fine. I think I love the Snake.

I rounded the corner to The Tasty Tart with delicious thoughts of my sexy man swirling around my head and—*holy crap.*

Look at that line.

"Petyr! Mira!" I bellowed.

My young assistant nearly skidded into the back room, hair in a messy bun, eyes wide.

My familiar was nowhere to be seen, but that was okay. Petyr worked on his own schedule.

"Mira, can you please unlock the doors before the first customer has an aneurysm?" I muttered, jerking my thumb toward the front.

The folks of Castor's Corner took their carbs

very seriously. Being even one minute late to open was practically an act of war.

Already, an old Wizard with a gap in his front teeth was trying to magic a few croissants out of the display case.

His spell fizzled, popped, and then zapped him square on the butt.

"Is this how you treat your clients, missy?!" he yelped, rubbing his singed rear.

"If my clients try to steal from me, then yeah, this is exactly how I treat them," I shot back.

Petyr snarled from somewhere below counter-level—he was too short to see over the glass, but I appreciated the backup.

The little Domovyk showed up after all. My Witchy heart warmed at his timely appearance.

And even cooler, his magic had a sting to it.

Thievery was one of his top ten mortal sins.

I straightened, pasted on my business-owner smile, and addressed the three dozen sugar-starved townsfolk now crowding the doorway.

"Ladies and gents, I apologize for the delay. We had another incident in the wee hours, and we're running just a touch behind schedule. Mira and Petyr will get to you in an orderly fashion. Please remain calm, and no hexing. Thank you."

That earned me a few blinks, some muttering, and—miracle of miracles—orderly behavior.

No more glass door rattling.

No more greasy fingerprints on my otherwise spotless windows.

Blessed silence, well, as silent as Castor's Corner ever got before eight in the morning.

Now, without all that noise, a Witch could actually get some work done.

And Goddess knew these pastries weren't going to bake themselves.

Okay, technically, I could make them bake themselves—but that took precise focus.

And precision was something my magic hadn't been great at lately.

Until now.

Until him.

Ugh, I didn't even have to say his name for my heart to do that stupid flutter thing.

Conrad—the too sexy for his own good, and mine, troublemaker himself.

Man currently occupying far too much space in my head and—if I was being honest—my heart.

My maybe mate.

Ever since I'd stopped actively shoving away the thought that maybe, possibly, the Fates were right and he was my mate, my magic felt different. Lighter. Like it had shifted.

I was now eighteen hours without any random hardtack explosions.

And seeing how things were going lately, that was a feat!

Now, the energy inside me felt steady.

Smooth.

Like all my magic had been quietly waiting for me to pull my head out of my own butt and admit what my heart already knew.

I could feel it in the way my hands tingled when I shaped the dough, the way my kitchen seemed brighter, like the whole space was humming in approval.

When I sent a spell into the ovens to make the muffins rise just-so, the magic didn't sputter—*it sang.*

When I coaxed the fryers to hold the perfect temperature, it was like my will slid into the machinery without resistance.

Focus. Flow. Power.

All mine.

"You ready, my Witchy?" Petyr asked from beside me, his beady little eyes gleaming under his ridiculous *ushanka* hat.

"As I'll ever be," I replied, feeling a small, fierce smile tug at my lips.

Because if I could harness this new control in the kitchen, maybe—*just maybe*—I could use it to handle the bigger problems.

Like the bakery fires.

Like the furry little vandals Mrs. Gennaro had been screeching about.

Like the giant, coiled, maddeningly gorgeous problem named Conrad.

Was I ready?

The answer was simple—*I'm as ready as I'll ever be.*

CHAPTER TWENTY-FIVE-BELLA

BY THE TIME I joined Mira and Petyr on the floor, the rush was in full swing.

We were holding our own until Mrs. Gennaro stormed in like a one-woman tribunal, her purse swinging like a wrecking ball of judgment.

"Oh boy," I muttered under my breath, steeling myself for whatever she was bringing to my doorstep.

"Miss Strega," she said, her tone sharp enough to slice a lemon in midair.

"Mrs. Gennaro," I replied, smile cranked to *Customer Service Setting #7: Genuine but Guarded.*

"I had to come in personally to tell you the pastries you boxed for me the other night were outstanding."

My smile faltered. "Oh?"

"Yes. No issues there. However—"

Her eyes narrowed.

Like a hawk spotting prey.

"Since you are part of the Trifecta protecting our town, I am laying this complaint directly on your doorstep."

"What complaint? We fortified the wards on time —*no mess ups*—"

She waved a hand, cutting me off.

"Something is wrong, I tell you. And you'd think a complaint filed by the Vice President of the Castor's Corner Charmed Embers Women and Witches Social Club would be taken seriously!"

"A complaint from *who*? About *what*?"

"Ask our illustrious mayor. Who, by the way, is not seeing anyone this morning. Not even me! Seems she's taken ill, rather suddenly. Faking, if you ask me. Too cowardly to show her face. I swear you young Witches have none of the fortitude of Witches from my time."

I gritted my teeth so hard I was in danger of grinding down enamel.

Evie? Cowardly? Ha!

The woman had faced down Werewolves, rogue Trolls, Ghosts, Warlocks, Wizards, and a very angry cupcake Golem last spring—*okay, that last bit was kinda my fault.*

It was a Halloween cake order gone haywire—*anywho.*

It didn't matter because no one was going to talk about one of my oldest and dearest friends—*my cousin, my shero, my ride or die*—in front of me like that!

Then everything slowed.

Mrs. Gennaro's words sent my brain spinning.

Evie ill? Not seeing anyone?

I'd bet my best piping tips, it wasn't any regular illness.

"Oh my!" I whispered.

Yep. This was different from a common cold.

This was more like a certain *blessing in progress.*

And in a few months?

Well, I was willing to bet my Grandma's secret Easter panettone recipe there'd be a brand new Baby Castor.

Which made me grin. A lot.

I was going to be such a good Auntie Bella!

Well, cousin-by-blood, but titles were flexible when baked goods were involved.

"The stories I could tell you," Mrs. Gennaro continued, and I realized I'd missed, oh, probably a solid three minutes of whatever she'd been yammering about.

Oops.

Sorry not sorry.

"Anyway, that's not the issue. The past is in the past, but it's your behinds not doing your due duty— are you listening to me?"

I blinked.

Was she talking about *doody* or *duty*?

Because tone-wise, she could've gone either way.

I closed my eyes and silently begged the Goddess for patience.

Dealing with the elderly in Castor's Corner was never boring, but it was rarely straightforward.

They liked their conversations like they liked their quilt squares—meandering, mismatched, and occasionally sewn together with curse words.

"Now, my Great-Grandfather used to be the Deputy here," she went on, oblivious to my inner monologue.

"How nice," I murmured.

"Full of stories, he was. Anytime the town was under attack, the residents would band together under a Castor and run the troublemakers right out! Those were the good old days. When we had leaders with backbone and we knew who wore the pants around here," she said in a surprisingly misogynistic turn of events.

I scoffed.

She ignored me and continued.

"And then, of course, they'd string up the trespassers. Why, you can still find the purse and book bound in the human skins of those who dared enter our town with ill purposes on their evil little minds—"

"Dear Goddess," I murmured. "Does she have to keep saying skins and bowels in the same breath?"

My stomach did a little somersault.

I was a Witch who loved sugar, not gore.

You wanted a triple-chocolate mousse cake?

I was your girl.

You wanted tales of flayed invaders?

No, thank you. Please see Evie or Donny.

"Mrs. Gennaro," I tried, "there haven't been any trespassers—"

"No trespassers?" she screeched. "Then who do you think has been messing up lawns? Raiding garbage cans and dumpsters all over town? Not to mention, setting fire to your shop on a few separate occasions! Why, my very own Mr. Snugglesby won't leave my purse!"

She hoisted said purse, inside of which sat a

scraggly lapdog wearing two pink bows and the judgmental stare of a thousand ancestors.

Okay, I might have been just a little concerned before, but her list of weirdness made my pulse kick.

Because, messed up lawns? Dumpster raids? That sounded like a problem for the Sheriff, Parks & Recreation, and possibly the Sanitation Department.

But arson? Setting fires to businesses where anyone could have gotten hurt?

Now that was something else. And it was starting to sound suspiciously like my recent bakery mishaps weren't just bad luck or prankster teens.

What if someone really was targeting me?

"Okay," I said, pasting on my responsible business owner smile. "Come with me to my office. Mr. Snugglesby can have a treat while you, um, explain."

She puffed up like I'd just announced her as guest of honor at the Winter Solstice Ball.

"It's about time I be treated in a manner befitting my station."

Behind her, Mira caught my eye. The poor girl was trying to ring up a latte for a customer while silently mouthing, *Save me.*

I mouthed back, *Call Evie and Donny.*

A quick nod, and I ushered Mrs. G and her geriatric fluff ball toward my office.

I conjured a peanut-butter biscuit for Snugglesby (*note to self: launch a pet-treat line*) and settled in to hear her out.

She didn't disappoint.

Out came a binder the size of a grimoire, filled with grainy, black-and-white security footage printouts.

Then a laptop.

Then, I kid you not, taped testimonies from other cranky old-timers in town.

What was this woman's purse made of? Narnia leather? Remnants from an English Nanny's old carpetbag?

"Don't be rude," she snapped, catching me peering into the bag.

My cheeks went hot like I'd been caught stealing cookies from my own bakery.

A few minutes later, Donny bustled in with Mrs. Fox in tow (mid-hair foils), followed by Evie looking about as green as pistachio gelato and clutching a bucket.

"Oh my Goddess, Evie, sit down! You look like hell," I shot up, trying to push a chair under her before she fell.

"I can't keep anything down," she mumbled miserably.

Mrs. Gennaro sniffed like Evie's vomiting was somehow a personal insult.

"Guess you really are sick."

"Um," I tried again, "Mrs. Gennaro, these are my cousins—"

"They know me," she cut in. "I'm Vice President of the Charmed Embers Women and Witches Social Club."

Donny and Evie exchanged blank looks, then nodded like bobbleheads.

Mrs. Fox, however, didn't get the memo.

"Who?"

"Shh!" Donny hissed.

"Mrs. G seems to think we've been, um, *lax* in our *duties.*"

Snickers all around.

Because we were mature professionals.

Totally not laughing at the insinuation of laxatives and doodies.

Mrs. G rolled her eyes.

"Let's get on with it."

She hit play on her laptop, and we all crowded in.

The footage was garbage quality, but even through the static, I saw them.

Little, furry, not-of-this-world critters darting around in the dead of night—*chewing plants, knocking over bins, and, oh look, setting trash alight like it was the Vampire's Midsummer's Eve Rave & Rotisserie Weekend.*

"No way," Donny whispered.

"They can't do that," Evie gasped before bolting for the bathroom again.

Mrs. Fox narrowed her eyes.

"Those furry little cretins! I knew it wasn't my Johnny eating my marigolds."

I stared at the screen, my gut twisting.

This could be the connection.

Maybe all my so-called "bad luck" wasn't random after all.

And if that was true, I had a much bigger problem than burned aprons and broken glass display cases.

When Mrs. G finally swept out with Snugglesby in her tote, I turned to Donny and Evie.

"I think we need some advice from the big guns."

"I think you're right," Donny said grimly.

"What's going on?" Evie asked, holding a towel to her head.

"I'll explain after. Right now, I think we better set up a Swoosh call from your place, Evie."

We joined hands, ready to teleport, and for the first time in a long while, I felt *steady*.

Like the ground under my feet wasn't just mine—it was ours.

My besties, my cousins, my girls had my back. And I had theirs,

It felt good to know that. And then I felt even better because maybe—*just maybe*—I was finally ready to let Conrad in. To let him have my back, too.

He wasn't Jameson Vorhees or any of the other losers who'd made me feel small.

He was patient. He was protective.

And he had literally wrapped himself around me like he was keeping me safe from the whole damn world.

If these critters wanted to burn down my bakery, run amok in Castor's Corner, well, they were in for a fight.

Because I had magic, my girls, and one very determined smexy Snake Shifter who wasn't going anywhere.

This was my town, and I was going to do everything I could to defend it.

CHAPTER TWENTY-SIX-BELLA

SECOND SWOOSH CALL

The three of us—*me, Donny, and Evie*—linked hands over Evie's office desk, the computer monitor glowed between us, and the faint fizz of magic sparked where our fingers touched.

The air shimmered like heat over asphalt, the scent of espresso and woodsmoke swirling around us as the connection formed.

"La Befana?" Evie's voice rang out as the magic line solidified.

"It's Evie Castor from Castor's Corner."

Pause.

"Is that you Crafter's Coven? The picture is grainy. Amber, come fix this thing!" Magdelena, *aka La Befana*, shouted unnecessarily loudly.

"No, not Crafter's Coven. CASTOR'S CORNER." My lips tightened.

"Okay, there you are! Yeah, yeah, Castor's Cove—what's up?"

"Corner, okay, well, remember how we called you about the bakery fires the other day?"

Donny and I both leaned in closer, trying to catch the muffled, papery rasp of Magdelena's voice on the other end.

"Yep. So, I understand you have new firefighters. What's the problem? Their hoses get stuck?" she demanded.

"Um, no. No problem!" Evie said quickly, her Mayor Voice sliding into place. "They're great. Absolutely great. But there's been some, uh, other things happening around town."

I elbowed her.

"Menaces," I stage-whispered. "Mystery menaces."

Evie waved me off.

"We were wondering if you were aware of any heightened activity in other supernatural communities lately?"

"Well now that you mention it," La Befana drawled, "I recall seeing an uptick in complaints about missing pets and—*oh*—what was it? Ah yes, some property damage. Are the Hobgoblins trying out new recipes again?"

Donny paled. "Um, I hope not. Last time they 'tried new recipes,' someone's cat turned neon green and meowed 'YMCA' for a week."

"I liked that cat," I muttered.

"Look," La Befana cut in, "Karen's Kruegers is just going to have to solve this one alone. I can't do everything!"

And just like that—click.

She hung up.

The three of us stared at each other, our magical link dissipating into harmless sparkles.

"Well," I said, deadpan. "That went swimmingly. We're on our own."

How the hell are we supposed to solve this thing without help? I thought and groaned, slumping in my chair.

Before I could answer, a familiar low rumble curled around my ears.

"You're not alone, sweet Witch."

I turned to see Conrad filling the doorway like six and a half feet of trouble wrapped in dark denim and snake-smirk.

His green eyes glinted, and—yep—he was reading my mind again.

And for once, I was okay with it.

"*You* have *us*," Jaxson added, strolling in with Wolf swagger.

Ryan followed, holding a box that smelled suspiciously like chocolate croissants. "And snacks."

"Okay," I said, straightening in my seat. "Trifecta and Shifter backup. Mystery menaces don't stand a chance."

"Damn straight!" Conrad added.

And for the first time in a long while, everything felt just right.

CHAPTER TWENTY-SEVEN-BELLA

"ARE WE REALLY FOLLOWING THIS PLAN?" I asked, uncertainty ringing in my voice.

"Yes. It's a good plan, one sanctioned by Magdelena herself," Donny whispered.

"I'm gonna be sick," Evie added, unhelpfully.

"We told you to stay home!"

"No way would I do that to you guys. We're a team, a Trifecta. We do this together," she said, breaking off with a cough and dry heave.

The three of us huddled inside a replica dumpster behind the bakery.

The inside was completely clean, of course. I mean, no way would any of us have crouched inside a real one.

Bad enough I had to worry about Evie inside this

thing, but she'd insisted and by all accounts, Jaxson had still not told her about her condition.

I'd given the Wolf an ultimatum.

He had till Solstice Eve, after that I was breaking the news.

"Stay close, my Witchy," Petyr whispered, and I nodded at him.

Good thing our Domovyks were so fiercely protective of us.

The three little fury dudes refused to part from us, concerned we could be hurt.

They used their powers and cloaked us from the mystery menace that had come to our town.

We didn't know why they were here, but clearly, they had a bone to pick. It was about time we found out what their deal was. And soon. I had other fish to fry.

Conrad and I still needed to have our chat, but first, I had Trifecta business. When Mrs. Gennaro had entered my store, I had no idea the old Witch had something important to tell me.

Never judge a book, or a Witch, by its cover—another of Granny's infamous sayings.

There were a lot of things wrong with this little undercover operation of ours.

First, trying to catch an arsonist in the act was probably dumb, not to mention dangerous.

Second, we didn't know if they would even try again so soon.

Third, I was pretty sure I was in love with a Shifter, and I wanted him to mark me with his mating bite, and all of that scared the crap out of me.

Okay, my third point had nothing to do with the operation or the arsonist at all, but it weighed heavily on my mind.

What if Conrad was only fond of the chase? What if me saying no was what turned him on?

All I knew was it was way past time I stopped being afraid of going after the things I wanted.

And I wanted Conrad.

There, I admitted it.

I was just going to have to grab my big girl panties and take that leap of faith—*as soon as we finished this sting operation we had going on, I would.*

But all of those thoughts came to a screeching halt once I heard the sound of skittering outside the dumpster.

"What's that sound?" Donny asked.

"Shh," I whispered, straining my ears to hear.

"Ready?" Petyr asked me as the scratching noises got louder.

Something or things were on top of the dumpster, and they were attempting to open the lid.

Eeek!

We crouched in the not-a-dumpster—*seriously, it was a magically enhanced industrial compost bin, but fine, semantics*—holding our breaths while the moonlight threw shadows across the alley.

My thighs were cramping, Donny's hair was glowing faintly like a cursed neon sign, and Evie kept muttering about how she was "too nauseous for this nonsense."

Then we heard it.

First came the hisses—*long, drawn-out ones, like angry tea kettles*—and then grunts that sounded *furry.*

Not your average raccoon-scuffling-in-the-trash furry, but something bigger.

Then came the voices.

Yep, they could talk.

So that was a big fat no to the whole wild animal theory.

"Hey yo, Razor Paws, this here new fan-dangled dumpster top is stuck," an oddly deep voice mumbled, like a mobster raccoon who'd gargled gravel for breakfast.

"Quiet down, Two Fangs. We needs to set fire

before the Draco camera tags our sumptuous round asses," another replied.

I blinked at Evie.

"Sumptuous round asses?" I mouthed.

She shrugged. "Sounds architectural and decadent?"

"Why you two furry jackoffs still yapping?" a distinctly female voice chimed in.

"Hurry your fluffy asses up. These Witches gotta pay for what they did. No one messes with the Etherworld Fantastic Feline Familiar Union!"

"You got that right, Trashcan Sally. EFFFU is da bomb!" the first one added proudly.

Evie's eyes went wide.

"FU?" she whispered.

"That's it," I said, my patience officially hitting the done button. "Now!"

We didn't just hit them with magic—*we blasted them.*

A rush of teal, gold, white, and pink magic shot from our fingers, curling together into one massive wave that made the bin's plastic lid shiver like Jell-O before lifting straight into the air.

The three on top—*now fluffy flailing silhouettes against the moon*—howled, hissed, and yelled things like *"My tail!"* and *"Don't look at me, I'm naked without my smoke cloak!"*

We were just getting started.

CHAPTER TWENTY-EIGHT-BELLA

"GODDESS OF POWER,
Hear our plea,
Villainous hearts,
Shall never see,
Castor's Corner as a place,
To infiltrate and deface.
Keep our neighbors,
Safe and free,
As we will, mote it be."

The words rolled out of us like muscle memory, the Trifecta's magic surging and sparking around our bodies until the air smelled like roasted marshmallows and ozone.

Our Domovyks—*Gryn, Ivan, and Petyr*—zipped

into view, their little magical bodies glowing, reinforcing the spell.

The polymers of the plastic lid morphed into pure steel, snapping shut with a clang that sent the vandals inside into another chorus of offended screeches.

Jaxson, Ryan, and Conrad appeared at the end of the alley, moving fast but not charging in.

They'd been waiting in the shadows just in case—and the fact they were letting us handle it while still ready to step in?

Yeah, that hit me right in the feels.

"You got that right, Sugar," Conrad said with that slow, devastating grin of his.

He was pointing some kind of weapon at the steel bin like he'd been born to protect me.

Like a cross between a magic wand and an AK-47.

I didn't even care that he'd read my mind again.

For the first time, it felt *safe*.

Comforting, even.

Ermagerd. I was in so much trouble.

I turned back to the bin now prison, *aka magically impossible to break out of pet crate*.

"Alright, you three, you've got a lot of explaining to do."

There was a pause, then a simultaneous *"Meoowww?"* from inside.

The steel shimmered, the magic lock flaring just enough for us to get a peek—and that's when Evie screeched, "Cats? You're just *cats*!?"

Sure enough, three furious, floofy cats stared back at us.

One was wearing a tiny leather vest that read Vice President, EFFFU, another had on a rhinestone collar that spelled "Two Fangs," and the third—a sleek black she-cat—had eyeliner so sharp it could cut glass.

"Oh, you Witches are gonna pay," Two Fangs growled. "You don't mess with the EFFFU."

I threw up my hands. "Seriously? All this chaos because you guys are in a cat gang?"

"Correction," the she-cat said with a sniff, "an *elite* cat gang."

Donny deadpanned, "We got punk'd by militant house pets."

Ryan choked back a laugh.

Jaxson outright lost it.

Conrad, though?

He just stepped closer to me, brushed his hand against mine, and murmured, "Don't worry, Sugar. They're all hiss and no claws."

Except judging by the murderous glare the she-cat gave me, I wasn't so sure.

"Evie, you saw the footage," Donny said.

"I was puking my head off at the time, Donny. Forgive me for missing out," she mumbled.

"You okay, Darlin'?" Jaxson asked, holstering his gun before gathering her close.

"Yeah, I just can't shake this stomach bug," she told him.

"Actually, Evie—"

"Not the time," I interrupted.

"Okay, you three, spill. What is your beef with Castor's Corner? And me, what is your beef with *me*?"

The three angry felines hissed and spit for two whole minutes before I zapped them with an extra-large dose of hardtack.

The stuff filled the interior of the cage, giving the little fuckers barely any room to move or breathe.

"Ouch! Okay, okay, we'll talk!" the female shouted.

"We are here to represent the Etherworld Feline Familiar Union, EFFU for short."

"Why are you saying FU, shouldn't it be E F F U?" Donny asked.

"What she talking about?" Razor Paws mumbled to Two Fangs.

"Witches aren't known for their smarts," he told his fellow feline, and I added a little more hardtack to the cage.

"Ouch! Stop. Please!"

I'd caught the male cats' names, but the female's name, I did not know. And I didn't care.

"Leave them to us," Petyr snarled. "We will take care of these vile felines! You who vowed to protect Witches and have been harming them shall pay for your misdeeds!"

"Actually," I told him. "You don't have to do that, Petyr. We've contacted La Befana, herself, and these three are going to get exactly what they deserve."

"La Befana? Nooooooo!" they howled.

Just then, an enormous BOOM sounded.

The shuffling of little paws had me, Donny, Evie, our boys, and the three Domovyks turning around to welcome our new arrivals.

"Alright, where's the funky felines at?" a large Maine coon with a brindle coat and a collar that read Marcus Aurelius Felinibus asked.

"That's them alright. Dang EFFU reps causing a fussssss," Esteban Notail added.

"We gots it from here, youz fine Trifecta badasses," Fluffy Iglesias said.

"Thank you. I was hoping to hear why they did this."

"*We'll never tell you treachoroussss Witchessss,*" the female mumbled. It was hard to hear since she and her two companions were smashed against the bars from all the hardtack piled inside the cage.

"Dats easy," Fluffy Iglesias continued.

"EFFU is a non-authorized organization of feline familiars wanting to control what kinds of familiars go to Witches. They's what you call *fanatsics* and shit. They's don't respect the supernatural order, and now, we got the three worst bandits thanks to you's three smokin' hot females."

"Watch it," Jaxson muttered.

"No foul, Wolf daddy. Just remarking on they fine assetssss," Esteban Notail said.

I grinned at the three infamous familiars—they worked for La Befana herself—and I thanked them with a couple of boxes of my new Peanut Butter Bacon Delights before they took off with the EFFU crew.

"Please make sure Magdelena and Drusilla get the small boxes of goodies. The three big ones are for you three," I said, handing the large pile of bakery boxes to Esteban Notail, who started drooling immediately.

"Thank you very much, Bellicious," Fluffy Iglesias replied. "The goods shall be delivered to those two badasses Witch bosses pronto. Let's go, boyzz!"

After we signed off on the capture and scribbled our sworn affidavits—*because apparently Witch justice still required paperwork*—Jaxson Swooshed the whole report (complete with magical mugshots) to La Befana herself.

Good riddance.

That was one magical mess I was thrilled to see handled.

Those fur-coated hooligans had been attacking my shop, for Goddess's sake.

My shop.

I don't care if you're a magical familiar or the personification of Karma itself, you don't mess with my tarts.

Truth be told, I wasn't sure how much more of it I could have taken.

Jealousy and misplaced righteousness were ugly beasts on their own—*add claws, fangs, and a union card, and you had a recipe for chaos.*

We were lucky we stepped in before anyone— Witch, Shifter, or feline—got hurt.

Petyr was getting the night off to Swoosh-call his family, which was sweet, so I told him to take the whole house to himself.

He immediately invited Gryn and Ivan over for an evening of *preferans*, vodka, and hardtack.

Because apparently nothing says "relaxation" like a full Slavic familiar bro-night.

"Well, that's that," Evie said with a satisfied sigh, brushing her palms like she'd just vanquished evil and folded the laundry.

"Come on, Darlin'," Jaxson drawled, scooping her up bridal-style like the overgrown, muscle-bound wolf prince he was. "Let's go home."

Ryan glanced my way, one big arm wrapped possessively around Donny. "Unless you need us to stick around and clean up, Bella?"

I shook my head. "Nothing to clean. They never made it inside."

Then I exhaled.

Hard.

My whole body felt lighter.

Then Conrad stepped forward, hand extended.

"Shall we?"

There was something about the way he asked— *gentle, but firm.*

Like the invitation was really a promise.

I didn't hesitate. I slipped my hand into his, my palm tingling instantly, and my heart decided to throw a parade in my chest.

"Do you mean it, Bella?" His green eyes glowed in that way that made me want to fan myself and check if my lipstick was still intact.

I smiled, feeling the decision settle deep in my bones.

"I mean it, Big Guy."

The corner of his mouth curved in a slow, sinful smile.

"Then let's go home so I can finally claim you, Sugar."

And just like that, I was ready to take the leap. Tonight.

No magic spell, no divine sign—just me, my Snake Shifter, and a leap of faith towards a future that suddenly didn't feel so scary.

CHAPTER TWENTY-NINE-
CONRAD

I STILL COULDN'T BELIEVE it. This whole time cats were behind every attempted arson and vandalization.

Not rival Shifters.

Not a Dark Witch Coven.

Or Supernatural Assassins.

Cats.

But as Bella and I walked arm in arm down the moonlit street, the air still thrumming faintly from the magic she'd unleashed, it made a twisted kind of sense.

Displaced familiars whipped up into a frenzy over some half-baked belief that only felines could serve as true companions to Witches.

Jealousy, pride, and bad information—*a dangerous mix in any species.*

"I still can't believe they targeted *me*," Bella mused.

"You know, the three of you are pretty famous in the supernatural world, Sugar," I told her, squeezing her hand, needing her to know this wasn't just some small-town witch drama. "I'd heard of the Witch Trifecta before. I just never knew I'd be fated to one of you."

She tipped her head, her eyes searching mine, curious and wary all at once.

"And? How do you feel about that?"

I stopped us cold, turning so the lamplight hit her face, dusted with flour like stardust on warm skin.

My chest ached, my Python coiling tighter in my gut.

"I feel positively honored, sweet Bella. You're my mate. The only woman to ever call to my Python. I know it's soon, and you're a Witch, not a Shifter—it's different for you. But I love you. I will wait as long as it takes for you to accept my claim."

Her lips parted, the soft pink glistening in the cool night air.

"That might be sooner than you think," she whispered—and then her mouth was on mine.

The second our lips touched, the bond surged between us like a live wire.

Her magic slid into my senses—*warm and sweet, smelling faintly of sugar, vanilla, lemony citrus, and something older, wilder.*

It didn't just brush me.

It wrapped me up, tangling through my veins, stroking over every nerve ending until I felt drunk on her.

By the time we reached her home, made it to her bedroom, I was already half feral with need.

She peeled her clothes away and mine like she couldn't wait another second.

And I was so there for that.

Waving her hand, my sweet Witch cast a shedding spell that had us both down to our birthday suits, and my hands—fuck, my hands—couldn't decide where to land first.

The generous curve of her hips?

The plush softness of her breasts?

The silky weight of her hair?

It was like sensory overload, but I could handle it. Handle her.

Hell, I was born to do just that.

"Come here, Sugar," I hissed, sliding my tongue into her sweet mouth.

I traced the curves of her soft body lovingly, carefully, laying us both down atop her firm mattress.

"Need you, Conrad," she whimpered.

"You got me, Sugar."

Then I slid into her tight, wet sheath, and it wasn't just heat that surrounded me.

It was home.

Her body gripped me like she'd been forged around me, and my Python uncoiled in sheer, unrestrained satisfaction.

Somewhere in that rhythm—*thrust, gasp, kiss, sigh*—our souls brushed.

A spark leapt, not just in my chest but in my very marrow, like lightning striking ancient stone.

"I'm ready," she breathed, her voice breaking on a gasp.

Every instinct in me went still.

"Ready?"

Was it finally going to happen? Was she going to let me have her?

My Python coiled inside of me.

"Yes. Make me yours, Conrad."

My vision tunneled, all sound narrowing to the rush of my own blood.

"I can't take it back once I do this, Bella. You have to be sure."

My voice came out rough, the hiss of my other form weaving through it as I drove into her, slow and deep, testing her resolve.

"I'm positive, mate. Claim me," she moaned—and I felt her body clench around me, the first flutter of her climax already starting.

The Python inside me roared its approval.

My muscles trembled from holding back, but instinct took over.

I flexed my hips first, stroking that secret place inside her. The one that made her moan and clench tightly around my cock—making me want to explode.

But first, I struck—fast, precise—my fangs sinking into the curve where her neck met her shoulder. Her blood hit my tongue like a shot of pure magic, molten honey laced with lightning, and I swear the earth itself tilted.

Pain flashed through her for a heartbeat—*then melted into pleasure so intense I felt it ripple through the bond like a tidal wave.*

Her orgasm slammed through her and into me, dragging me under.

Oh, but I went willingly.

This little Witch had me in her grasp and I never ever wanted to leave.

Every pulse of her body was a fist clenching around my cock, milking me, claiming me right back.

Mate. Love. Mate. Love. MATE. LOVE. LOVE. LOVE.

Her voice and mine echoed together—*inside my head or aloud I wasn't quite sure*—chanting the truth into my bones.

But I wasn't just claiming her with my bite.

Bella was claiming me right back, and I never felt so honored. *So humbled. So ecstatic.*

Her magic didn't just wrap around me—*it poured into me*, flooding every hollow space inside until I felt too full, too lit, too alive to ever be the same again.

It coiled around my Python, stroking, binding, sealing us together in a knot that could never be untied.

I filled her in hot, pulsing waves, the release shuddering through me in endless rolls until my arms shook from holding her so tight.

"You're finally mine, sweet Witch," I murmured against her lips, tasting her, my voice nothing but gravel and reverence.

She nipped at me, that wicked little smirk making my cock twitch hard inside her again.

"I like it when you're bitey," I warned, even as she pushed at my chest and flipped us, straddling me like she owned the world.

"Good, cause I'm not done with you yet. Now roll over, it's my turn to ride, Snake Man."

"Anything you want, mate," I promised, my hands gripping her hips, guiding her down on me again.

The bond pulsed between us with every move, her magic, and my Shifter heat winding tighter, hotter, until there was no telling where I ended and she began.

"Come with me, Bella," I groaned, feeling her walls flutter again. "Let's find our forever together."

"Yes," she gasped—and then we were gone again, into the spiral of heat and magic and inevitability that would be our lives from this moment on.

Mine. Mate.

CHAPTER THIRTY-BELLA

THE CASTOR'S Corner Summer Solstice Festival was the kind of event that made outsiders shake their heads and locals beam with pride.

By mayoral decree—*Evie's own, which she announced with all the pomp and sass of a royal proclamation*—Main Street was blocked off, transformed into a kaleidoscope of color and chaos.

Rows of tents spilled over with carnival games, glittering jewelry, magically-infused crafts, and enough fried food to tempt even the most iron-stomached Werewolf.

Hangman's Field was decked out like a midway fever dream—Ferris wheel glowing like a halo, tilt-a-whirl flashing in rainbow bursts, and every supernatural—*even a few members of the giant race, the Dark*

Elves, relatives of townsfolk who'd been accidentally invited—out enjoying themselves.

The festivities had started at noon and wouldn't stop until the moon was kissing dawn.

My bakery had a prime tent spot, and I had six employees scheduled—two inside the bakery for the stragglers who wanted their pastries "fresh from the oven" and four manning the tent.

Mira was in charge, clipboard in hand, ponytail bouncing like she was auditioning for "Most Enthusiastic Witch Alive." Girl had stepped up in a big way.

By eleven-thirty, my role shifted from vendor queen to mission critical maid of honor.

I had just thirty minutes to get the pièce de résistance—*the final cake for Evie and Donny's joint wedding ceremony*—delivered to the clearing before the vows began.

The cake was a towering vision of sugar and artistry—too many tiers to count, white fondant so smooth it could've been sculpted from porcelain, piped lacework, pale blush sugar roses climbing up the side like a romantic fairytale vine.

I wasn't nervous about the cake. The cake was perfect.

No, the nerves were about what came after.

"You ready, my Witchy?" Petyr asked, appearing at my elbow in his best magical formalwear—*a tiny waistcoat and a bow tie so sparkly it might have been enchanted to outshine the moon.*

I nodded, my stomach twisting in excitement and panic.

Ivan and Gryn joined him, both with the smug expressions of magical familiars who knew exactly how to pull off a high-profile pastry delivery.

In a coordinated shimmer of teal, gold, and pearl light, the three Domovyks whisked the cake away, reappearing seconds later beneath the designated wedding tent.

I rattled off last-minute instructions to my crew, then took a deep breath and headed for the clearing alone.

Somewhere out there, Conrad was with Jaxson and Ryan, the two grooms-to-be.

I could picture him—*broad shoulders, that easy green-eyed grin, probably making some low rumble in his chest that I'd feel in places no rumble had business reaching.*

And if the Goddess was kind, he wouldn't object to what I was about to do.

The clearing opened up before me in a whirl of

music, laughter, and the shimmer of fairy lights strung through the trees.

Evie and Donny stood at the edge of the aisle, resplendent.

Evie's gown was rockabilly perfection—*a halter-top bodice, crisp white with a bright aqua petticoat peeking out beneath the mid-length skirt*—and it completely disguised her tiny baby bump which I still didn't know if she knew about yet.

But that was for me to find out later.

Her hair was swept into victory rolls, and her accessories matched down to the enamel pin on her bouquet handle.

She looked like she could strut straight from the altar to a pin-up calendar shoot.

Donny's gown was the polar opposite—a sleek, mermaid silhouette with a train so dramatic it needed its own zip code.

Chantilly lace veil.

Red lips.

Red nails.

Glittering shoes.

And her hair—blonde waves so perfect it looked like every shampoo commercial ever filmed had been distilled into one Witch.

"Well?" Donny arched a brow at me. "Aren't you going to put it on?"

I stared at the white-and-pale-pink confection she gestured to, my heartbeat doing double-time.

This was it.

My moment of truth.

Was I the timid baker who hid behind her counter when things got too real?

Or was I the woman who took a leap of faith, consequences be damned, and went for the gold?

The first strains of the wedding march drifted over the clearing. I swallowed hard.

My hands trembled.

"I won't know unless I try," I murmured.

"Great! No time to do this the old-fashioned way," Evie said with a wicked grin.

Her fingers wiggled, and before I could protest— shoomp—magic wrapped me in a shimmer of gold and rose.

When it cleared, I gasped.

I was a walking, talking wedding day fantasy.

Full skirt, sweetheart neckline, bodice hugging my curves like it had been stitched there by the Goddess herself.

My hair was a cascade of glossy curls, a delicate

circlet nestled like it had been waiting for me all my life.

My cheeks flushed, my lips tinted the perfect pink, and my neckline, well.

Let's just say Conrad was going to need a moment.

"Buxom beauty at its best," Donny said, smirking.

"Oh, I needed to apologize for something," I began, going for broke, "I mean, I'm so sorry I never made it—"

"Never made what?" Evie asked, brows arched.

"A guilt-free goodie for us," I admitted, my voice wobbly. "But I wanted you two to know I'm proud of us. I'm done trying to change what we look like to suit anybody else's expectations. We are the Trifecta, dang it, and the Goddess gave us our curves for a reason."

"Damn straight," Donny sniffled.

"It was sure fun trying out all those recipes though!" Evie snorted a laugh.

"I love us," I said, my chest swelling, my magic humming in agreement.

And somewhere out there, I could feel Conrad's answering warmth through the bond, like a promise that he was already on his way to find me.

EPILOGUE 1-BELLA

"LADIES, THE GROOMS ARE GETTING ANXIOUS—" Conrad stepped into our tent, voice low and warm as always.

Then he froze.

The grin slid right off his face, replaced by wide-eyed shock.

"Bella," he murmured.

Oh, Goddess help me.

There he was—six and a half feet plus of lethal, delicious Shifter male—wearing a perfectly tailored gray morning suit that hugged his broad shoulders and lean waist like it had been sewn just for him.

Which, knowing Donny's fashionista connections, it probably had.

His green eyes burned into me, and my knees wobbled.

I had to mentally order myself not to drool on my surprise wedding dress.

And, oh wow, the dress.

The dress I had not been planning to reveal until, well, later.

Instead, here I was, full skirt flaring, satin and lace whispering around me, hair all glossy curls with a tiny veil pinned just so—*looking like a Witch who'd just stepped out of a fated mates fairytale.*

"Oh wow. I guess, um, I am doing this now," I whisper-screamed, flicking a wild glance at Evie and Donny.

They both nodded like smug matchmakers, grins wide enough to split their faces.

My palms went damp. My heart tried to leap out of my chest.

"Okay," I started, my voice wobbly but getting stronger, "I was going to sort of propose in my regular dress, you know, in front of everyone, so you couldn't say no," I said and sucked in a shaky breath.

"You got this," Evie whispered.

"Time to take that leap, Hells Bells," Donny seconded.

My girls had my back, and judging from the gleam in my man's eyes, he did too.

"Okay, here goes. Conrad Boman, I love you," I said, and I meant it with all my heart.

"That's it." I giggled. "I love you, and I want to be with you forever—not just as your mate, but as your wife. If you need time, I underst—"

"Yes."

I blinked.

"Yes?"

"Yes," Conrad growl-hissed, crossing the space between us in three long strides. "Yes, with all my heart. I will marry you, sweet Witch. I wanna be yours, want you to be mine, until the end of time, and maybe even after that."

And then his arms were around me, pulling me so tight to his chest I could feel the deep, steady thrum of his heart against mine.

His mouth found mine in a kiss that wasn't just hot—it was the kind that melted every single shard of fear I'd ever carried about not being enough.

His love crashed into me like magic.

My own magic swirled up in answer, fizzing in champagne bubbles beneath my skin, wrapping around us in a shimmer I was too giddy to control.

By the time our kiss slowed, I was breathless, flushed, and absolutely, irrevocably his.

He rested his forehead against mine, voice low and certain.

"I'll be waiting for you at the altar, sweet Bella."

"Okay."

Tears pricked my eyes, but I managed a watery smile.

Turning to my cousins—*my best friends, my magical soul-sisters*—I bit my lip.

"So, I know I didn't ask, and this is your wedding day, and I'm sorry for totally crashing it, but I think it's supposed to be ours too. Promise you aren't mad?"

"Mad?" Donny scoffed, eyes shining. "Are you kidding me? This is the best thing ever. And I mean ever. Let's go get hitched, ladies!"

"Yes, let's," Evie agreed, sliding into the middle like she'd been choreographing this her whole life.

She linked arms with both of us, one hand on each.

"By the way, Jaxson told me the news—"

Her eyes went wide and she grinned.

"I swear I'm so embarrassed I didn't realize I was pregnant before you all did!"

"You are gonna be such a good mom!" Donny screeched.

"And this baby is gonna have the best aunties," I seconded.

Donny and I both burst out laughing, giggles tangled with happy tears as we started toward the altar in a slow, steady march.

And there they were.

Our men.

Our Shifters.

Our mates.

Looking so ridiculously good in their suits I half-expected some sort of magical law to be passed against it.

Broad shoulders, proud stances, smiles that lit up the clearing like another string of fairy lights.

My heart did that stupid fluttering thing again, and I didn't even care.

The bells tolled midnight just as we reached them.

La Befana herself—*Magdelena, long white robe flowing dramatically in the lantern light*—stood ready to bless not one, not two, but three unions.

"Okay, so, I just got ordained like half an hour

ago, but it's legal, so let's do this," she announced breezily. "Quick version, because I gotta fly back to Northern before my kids explode something."

I flipping adored that Witch.

"First up—Evie and Jax, do you promise to love, cherish, honor, and take care of each other for the rest of your lives?"

Um okay. So, it was gonna be a speed service.

"Yes."

"Yes."

"Fabulous. Rings? Great. You're married. Moving on."

She swung her gaze to Donny and Ryan. "You two wanna be hitched?"

"Yes!"

"Yes!"

"Boom. Married. Okay, last but not least—Bella and Conrad. I see this was last-second, but that's cool. Do the two of you promise to do all those things I already said? You know, be faithful, cherish, love, oh, and deliver a dozen Undeath By Chocolate cupcakes to me every month." She eyed us suspiciously.

"Um, okayyy," I murmured.

"Yes," Conrad said, voice rough with emotion.

"I promise to love, worship, cherish, and make

sure we send you any goodies you like *express*, La Befana, for as long as this beautiful Witch is mine."

Awwwwwww.

My heart felt so full it was practically overflowing into my magic, making the air around us sparkle faintly.

And when Magdelena finally said the words—"You're married"—I realized I'd just found my forever.

And it felt perfect.

EPILOGUE-2-CONRAD

"EXCELLENT! I now pronounce you three Witches and Shifters, husbands, and wives! Wait—*you're not married to everyone, just to your one mate*—oh Goddess! I forked this up. Look, you get me, right? Does everyone get me?" Magdelena's voice carried across the clearing.

There was a ripple of laughter, but my focus wasn't on her. My entire world was the woman standing beside me in a swirl of satin and lace.

"We get you," I said automatically, though I was looking straight at Bella, not our officiant.

She giggled—*Goddess, that sound*—and the tight coil in my chest loosened just enough to let me breathe again.

It was done.

She was mine.

Not just in the primal, Shifter-bond way that had been burning through my blood since the moment we met, but in every way that counted—*law, magic, body, heart, mind, and soul.*

Afterwards, the clearing erupted into hand-shakes, hugs, and congratulations.

Townsfolk and family swarmed us, and the three couples made our way to the center where the cake waited.

My mate's cake.

"Ready, my Witchy?" Petyr asked her, his Domovyk grin all mischief and pride.

She nodded, eyes bright, and he clapped his hands.

Silver mist burst into the night sky, scattering sparkles like falling stars.

And there it was—*her masterpiece.*

The crowd gasped.

Bella bit her lip like she was bracing for judg-ment, and my heart ached at how much she still didn't see what I saw—a miracle of a woman who could out-bake, out-magic, and outshine anyone in this town.

Evie and Donny didn't hesitate.

They threw themselves at her in a tackle-hug that nearly knocked her over.

"Oh, Bella, this is perfect!" Evie cried.

I looked at the cake and whistled.

The thing was massive, covering an entire table, and so detailed it could have been a miniature set for a magical movie.

"I figured, why go traditional when we are anything but?" Bella said, voice hesitant but proud.

"You made the entire town!" Evie gasped.

"And look at the toppers!" Donny squealed.

I leaned closer. Damn, she had thought of every-thing—*our shops, City Hall, every street, and lantern.*

Layers of Devil's food, lemon cake, carrot cake, vanilla swirl cake, and red velvet built the whole structure.

The fondant work was so perfect I half-expected the tiny windows to light up.

And in the center—our clearing.

Bonfire flickering with real, heatless flame she'd spelled herself.

Around it stood three tiny Witches—*Bella, Evie, and Donny*—and beside them, were *us*, their mates in human form.

Behind each of us, our Shifter forms.

Wolf.

Bear.

Python.

My chest tightened.

She'd put me there. Not just in man form, not just as her Shifter—but as part of us.

"It's perfect, Bella. Just like you," I murmured, leaning down to nuzzle the soft curve of her neck.

She shivered, and my Python uncoiled in smug satisfaction.

Then I slid my hand into my pocket and pulled out the band I'd been carrying for weeks.

Not flashy.

Not elaborate.

Just a solid, warm gold ring.

I took her hand, slid it onto her finger, and held it up so everyone could see.

Her eyes went wide. "Conrad—"

"I thought this would suit you for work," I said quietly.

And then she launched herself at me like she'd been waiting her whole life to do it.

"It's perfect!"

I caught her easily—my hands had been made to hold this woman.

Her laughter was in my ear, her scent in my lungs, her heartbeat pressed against mine.

Maybe leaps of faith are worth it after all.

"They sure are, Sugar," I told her, holding her close enough to feel the magic sparking between us. "And you can count on me to be there whenever you decide to jump. I will always catch you."

Her eyes softened, a mixture of mischief and something deeper. "I'll catch you too, Conrad," she promised.

Marriage was a new adventure for both me and my hungry Python.

Good thing my Witch was just as hungry for me.

And standing there with her in my arms—*veil tangled against my chest, perfume clinging to my suit, her soft curves molding perfectly into me*—I knew we were already exactly where we were meant to be.

"Damn straight. Let's go home," she whispered in my ear, voice low and warm enough to melt steel.

My Python went wild, hissing in my head like I'd just poured gasoline on him.

Home. Ours.

"You sure?" I murmured, because as much as I wanted to sprint out of here like a caveman, I needed her to say it.

"I'm sure, Big Guy," she said, those gorgeous eyes locking on mine. "I want you to take me home and make me yours."

Every instinct in me roared its approval.

The air between us snapped with magic and Shifter heat.

"I can do that. I love you, mate," I hissed, letting the word mate curl around us like a vow.

Before she could say another word, I bent, scooped her up, and hoisted her over my shoulder in a perfect fireman carry. She squealed—a sound halfway between shock and delight—*her laughter vibrating down my spine like music.*

"Bella!"

"You're gonna miss the cake!" Evie and Donny called after us, their voices muffled under the roar of applause and whistles from the crowd.

I didn't even slow down.

"No she won't," I called back over my shoulder. "Petyr, bring us a slice later, okay? Much later."

"For my Witchy, anything," the Domovyk replied, grinning like he'd just won a bet.

The night air was thick with summer—sweet fried dough from the festival still lingering, the hum of the rides spinning in the distance, the faint electric buzz of the wards around Main Street.

Bella's hand curled into the back of my shirt, her other arm tightening around my waist.

I could feel the heat of her magic pulsing in little

bursts against my back, answering the steady thrum of my own Shifter energy.

Life in Castor's Corner was never gonna be dull. I knew that for a fact. But right now? I didn't give a damn about magical trouble, mystery menaces, or tomorrow's chaos.

Tonight, she was going to be mine in every way the Fates had intended.

And nothing—*not cats or fires or Domovyks, hell, not even the Goddess herself*—was going to interrupt us.

"What's going on inside that head of yours?" she asked once I carried her over the threshold and made my way upstairs, placing her down gently on the bed.

"Just thinking how happy I am that you're finally mine, sweet Witch."

"Yeah? Show me."

Goddess, I loved it when she was demanding.

"I can do that," I hissed, and raised an eyebrow as she magicked away our clothes.

"You better, Big Guy. I'm counting on it."

EPILOGUE 3–BELLA

A FEW WEEKS *Later*

Summer was finally giving way to fall, and I was elbows deep in flour, sugar, and unapologetic joy.

The air in my bakery was thick with cinnamon and nutmeg, the kind of scents that wrapped around you like a cozy blanket and whispered, Yes, you should absolutely have another one.

I was in my happy place—testing new recipes, perfecting the old ones.

Apple cider donuts?

Divine.

Pumpkin muffins?

Basically an edible hug.

And not to brag (okay, maybe a little), but I made them better than anyone else.

Not conceit. Just facts.

But even better than all my plotting and planning for the season was the fact that, deep inside me, I felt settled.

For the first time in years, my magic wasn't fizzling or sputtering from stress—it hummed.

Warm. Steady. Certain.

Petyr, my ever-snarky Domovyk, had been helping me sharpen it too, teaching me old-school Witch tricks and whispering supernatural secrets I didn't even know existed.

(Seriously, some of those recipes from the old grimoires? Wild. One of them involved pickled frog toes. Don't ask.)

But most of all, I was grounded because of *him.*

My husband.

My mate.

My ridiculously sexy Snake man who I simply could not get enough of.

Conrad completed me in every way—mind, body, soul, and occasionally, snack preferences.

Seriously, it's hard to find someone who understands the true glory of ingredient combos like peanut butter bacon and lemon rose petal.

Anyway, I loved every second of our life together.

He was supportive in ways that mattered, and thoughtful in ways that floored me daily.

Flowers in my kitchen.

Notes tucked in my apron pocket.

A new whisk charmed to never clump batter.

And yes—I still had my girls.

The Witch Trifecta of Castor's Corner was as strong as ever.

Sure, we'd all gotten ourselves hitched to our fated Shifters, and yeah, our lives had changed in big ways. But the core truth hadn't shifted.

We were still besties.

Still cousins.

Still the magical chaos unit this town didn't deserve but desperately needed.

Things had actually been calm lately.

Well, calm for us.

Which naturally meant the phone decided to ring at that exact moment.

Uh-oh.

I grabbed it. "Bella here—"

"Bella! Come quick," Donny's voice blasted through the line. "Something's going down at the cemetery. There's an open interdimensional black hole, a giant Demogorgon slipped through, and Mrs. Fox's children need our help!"

"Again?" I sighed. "She really needs to keep those kids out of the graveyard."

"Tell her that after you save them," Donny snapped.

"Fine, fine, I'm on my way."

I popped my head into the kitchen.

"Mira, you're in charge! Trifecta business!"

She saluted with a wooden spoon, and I bolted out the front door just in time to see my sexy deputy husband screech to a halt in his cruiser, lights flashing.

He leaned across the passenger seat, green eyes sparkling.

"Need a ride, Sugar?"

I grinned, heart doing that stupid happy flip.

"You know I do, Big Guy."

"Hop on in."

And that was that.

I slid in beside him, the scent of leather and pine flooding my senses as he hit the gas.

Together, we rode off to do what we did best—join our friends, save the town, and maybe, maybe reward ourselves with something deep-fried and slathered in frosting after.

"Sounds good to me, Sugar," Conrad said, his grin pure trouble.

Yeah—life in Castor's Corner was perfect.

And it was only just beginning.

The end.

Thank you for reading my Hungry Fur Love series! I am so grateful for the opportunity to present these extended editions to you for the first time in eBook and print, and I can't wait to add more to the wonderful supernatural town of Castor's Corner!

If you want more Witchy madness, check out my Howlin' Good Fairytale Retellings here: https://www.cdgorri.com/series/a-howlin-good-fairytale-retelling/

Thank you for reading!

del mare alla stella,

C.D. Gorri

ALSO BY C.D. GORRI

<u>Paranormal Romance Books by Series</u>

A Howlin' Good Fairytale Retelling

Barvale Holiday Tales

Dire Wolf Mates

Hearts of Stone Series

Hungry Fur Love

Island Stripe Pride

Jersey Sure Shifters/EveL Worlds

Lords of Nightfall

Macconwood Pack Novel Series

Macconwood Pack Tales Series

Mated in Hope Falls

Moongate Island Tales

Motley Crewd Shifters

NYC Shifter Tales

Purely Paranormal Romance Books

Speed Dating with the Denizens of the Underworld

The Barvale Clan Tales

The Bear Claw Tales

The Falk Clan Tales

The Guardians of Chaos

The Maverick Pride Tales

The Wardens of Terra

Twice Mated Tales

When Worlds Collide

Witch Shifter Clan

Wyvern Protection Unit

<u>Young Adult/Urban Fantasy Books by Series</u>

Blackthorn Academy For Supernaturals

G'Witches Magical Mysteries Series
Co-written with P. Mattern

The Angela Tanner Files

The Grazi Kelly Novel Series

Witches of Westwood Academy

with Gina Kincade

<u>Contemporary Romance Books by Series & Title</u>

Carolina Rugby Romance

A Reason To Try

The Break Down

A Game of Ruck

Dump Tackle My Heart

Support Your Local Hooker

Sin Bin for the Billionaire

Cherry On Top Tales

Her Yule His Log

His Carrot Her Muffin

Her Chocolate His Bar

His Pickle Her Jam

Her Trick His Treat

His Wood Her Fire

Her Birthday His Package

Jersey Bad Boys

Merciful Lies

Devious Lies

Pitiful Lies

Mergers & Acquisitions

Desperate Measures

Desperate Needs

Desperate Desires

Desperate Actions

Desperate People

Desperate Crimes

Desperate Games

Desperate Secrets

Wild Billionaire Romance

His Wild Obsession

His Wild Temptation

His Wild Seduction

His Wild Attraction

Bonus Scene His Wild Halloween Night

Wrecked Rockstar Romance

Dirty Lyrics

Broken Chords

Wicked Beats

Be sure to check out my BUY DIRECT BUNDLES and get 30% off when you buy available only my website.

Click here for The Official C.D. Gorri Reading List - free download

ABOUT THE AUTHOR

USA Today Bestselling Author C.D. Gorri writes steamy Paranormal & Contemporary Romance and Urban Fantasy packed with heart, humor, and heat.

Join her mailing list here: https://www.cdgorri.com/newsletter

A lifelong book lover, she's rarely without a story in hand, and her own tales reflect that passion. Based in her beloved New Jersey, C.D. weaves the Garden State into many of her stories, grounding even the wildest supernatural adventures with a touch of home.

Her books are fast-paced, full of feels, and always end with a satisfying HEA. You'll meet sassy, curvy heroines and the possessive, love-driven heroes who adore them, whether they're Shifters, Vampires,

Witches, or just morally gray men falling hard in her contemporary worlds.

If you're into fated mates, fierce love, and action-packed romance where loyalty wins and love always triumphs then *welcome*. You're in the right place.

Thanks for reading!

Del mare alla stella,

C.D. Gorri

Curvy Heroines & Epic Heroes for the avid reader.
http://www.cdgorri.com
https://www.facebook.com/Cdgorribooks
https://www.bookbub.com/authors/c-d-gorri
https://twitter.com/cgor22
https://instagram.com/cdgorri/
https://www.goodreads.com/cdgorri
https://www.tiktok.com/@cdgorriauthor